A CHRISTMAS CAROL

ISBN 0 573 01070 6

A CHRISTMAS CAROL

Presented at the Playhouse Theatre, Buxton, on Tuesday, 21st December, 1948, with the following cast of characters :—

In the Prologue

A WOMAN	*Gwendoline Watford*
BOY	*Frederick Galyer*
1ST GIRL	*Barbara Leslie*
2ND GIRL	*Margaret Dale*

In the Play

EBENEEZER SCROOGE	*Nigel Arkwright*
BOB CRATCHIT	*Brown Derby*
FRED (SCROOGE'S NEPHEW)	*Richard Bebb*
1ST PORTLY GENTLEMAN	*Roy Leywood*
2ND PORTLY GENTLEMAN	*Will Leighton*
THE GHOST OF MARLEY	*Shaun Sutton*
THE SPIRIT OF CHRISTMAS PAST	*Barbara Leslie*
DANIEL	*Will Leighton*
FARMER GREENROW	*Charles Matthews*
MRS. GREENROW	*Carmen Hill*
SCROOGE AS A BOY	*Frederick Galyer*
MR. FEZZIWIG	*Roy Leywood*
DICK WILKINS	*John Bennett*
MRS. FEZZIWIG	*Jacqueline Barnett*
EMMA FEZZIWIG	*Margaret Dale*
FANNY FEZZIWIG	*Hazel Woodhouse*
DORA	*Christine Staley*
MARLEY AS A YOUNG MAN	*Shaun Sutton*
AUGUSTA	*Cynthia Leywood*
ADOLPHUS	*Charles Matthews*
THE SPIRIT OF CHRISTMAS PRESENT	*Peter Owen*
1ST COCKNEY	*Will Leighton*
2ND COCKNEY	*Harry Astelle*
TINY TIM	*Frederick Galyer*
AGNES (FRED'S WIFE)	*Gwendoline Watford*
THE SPIRIT OF CHRISTMAS TO COME	*Richard Bebb*
MRS. CRATCHIT	*Carmen Hill*
1ST BUSINESS MAN	*Shaun Sutton*
2ND BUSINESS MAN	*Harry Astelle*
3RD BUSINESS MAN	*Peter Owen*
LAD	*Patrick Freeman*
BELINDA CRATCHIT	*Barbara Leslie*
SARAH CRATCHIT	*Margaret Dale*
PETER CRATCHIT	*John Bennett*
MARTHA CRATCHIT	*Gwendoline Watford*

Produced by Shaun Sutton

NOTE. This cast may be reduced by the doubling of certain characters. See page 81.

SYNOPSIS OF SCENES

PROLOGUE

SCENE.—*A false proscenium runs across the stage about five feet above the setting line. There is a round arch at right angles to this proscenium on either side of the stage. A Traverse Curtain can be drawn behind the false proscenium to close in the forestage.*

(See the Ground Plan at the end of the Play.)

Before the CURTAIN *rises the carol "Good King Wenceslas" is sung off stage.*

The CURTAIN *rises on the last phrase of the carol and the* LIGHTS *fade in. The* TRAVERSE CURTAIN *is closed. Down* R. *is a wing armchair lit by warm firelight from a spot in the footlights. There is a burst of laughter off* L. *and a small* BOY *aged ten runs through the arch down* L. *and across to* R.C. *He carries a wooden sword and brandishes it. A* WOMAN *follows him to* C., *and two* GIRLS *run behind her. All wear modern clothes. The children wear paper hats and the* FIRST GIRL *carries a balloon.*

BOY (*waving his sword and chanting*). Look at me ! Look ! I'm the King ! (*He struts about down* R.)

FIRST GIRL. Kings don't have swords. They have crowns.

BOY. They have swords *and* crowns. (*He sings.*) " I'm the King of the Castle."

(The GIRLS *cross the* WOMAN *to* R. *and join in the song.)*

WOMAN. Quiet, children ! Granny's trying to rest. You'll wake her up.

(The CHILDREN *stop singing and turn to the* WOMAN.)

SECOND GIRL. Why is she resting ?

BOY. Did she have too much pudding ?

WOMAN (*laughing*). No !

BOY. I did !

WOMAN. She's just tired.

FIRST GIRL. She's awfully old.

BOY. I'm not old. (*He sings.*) " I'm the King of the Castle."

1

(*The* GIRLS *join in the song. The* BOY *marches right across the stage to down* L. *waving his sword. The* GIRLS *follow him in a single file.*)

WOMAN. Ssh! Quiet!

(*The* CHILDREN *stop singing. The* BOY *wheels about in silence and continues his heroic march across the stage to down* R. *The* GIRLS *stay* L.C.)

SECOND GIRL (*to the* FIRST GIRL). I ate more than you.
FIRST GIRL. You didn't. I had lots.
SECOND GIRL. I had more.
FIRST GIRL. You've got a bigger tummy.
SECOND GIRL (*indignant*). I haven't! (*She turns to the* WOMAN.) She says I've got a bigger tummy.
BOY (*stopping his antics with the sword and turning to the others*). I ate more than all of you. I had chicken and potatoes and stuffing and mince pies and greens and pudding and sweets and oranges and . . .
FIRST GIRL (*spitefully*). And a banana. I saw you take it off the sideboard when mummy wasn't looking.
BOY (*guiltily*). I didn't!
FIRST GIRL. Yes, you did! (*She chants.*) I saw you, I saw you!

(*The* SECOND GIRL *joins in.*)

WOMAN. Ssh! Poor Granny will wake up in a minute?
SECOND GIRL. Doesn't she want to see Father Christmas!
WOMAN. We'll go and tell her when he comes.
FIRST GIRL. *When* is he coming? (*She goes close to the* WOMAN.)
BOY } (*together*). { Yes, when? (*They also go to*
SECOND GIRL } { *the* WOMAN.)
WOMAN. Soon.
BOY. How soon?
WOMAN. In about half-an-hour.
FIRST GIRL. You said that half-an-hour ago.
WOMAN. It's no time at all if you don't think about it.
SECOND GIRL. Will he have a present for me?
BOY } (*together*). { And one for me, too?
FIRST GIRL } { Will he have one for me?
WOMAN (*shouting them down*). Yes. He'll have something for all of you.

2

SECOND GIRL. I wish he'd come now.

BOY. I'm going to show him my sword. (*He sings.*) " I'm the King of the Castle." (*He marches to down* L.)

(*The* GIRLS *join in, and follow him.*)

WOMAN. Children !

(*They stop singing, and turn to her.*)

Now listen, if you'll all be very good, and keep as quiet as this—(*She holds up her hand for complete silence*)—then I'll read you a story.

CHILDREN (*together*). Hurrah ! A story ! Oh, good !

WOMAN. Ssh ! Now, you promise to be quiet.

CHILDREN. Promise.

WOMAN. All right. (*She moves to the armchair and picks up a book that is lying on it.*) Now, come and sit round me. (*She sits.*)

(*The* CHILDREN *move to the armchair and sit on the floor around it.*)

That's it !

LIGHTING CUE. *The lights begin to fade, until only the chair is lit by a pool of firelight.*

FIRST GIRL. What's the story about ?

WOMAN. You'll see. (*She opens the book.*) It's in this book. And it's all about—guess what ?

(*The* CHILDREN *shake their heads.*)

It's all about Christmas.

(*They murmur excitedly.*)

BOY. Did you make it up ?

WOMAN. No. It was written years and years ago by a man called Dickens.

SECOND GIRL. My father knows him.

WOMAN. Oh, he can't.

SECOND GIRL (*persisting*). He does. I heard him say the other day " What the dickens are you talking about ? " He was awfully cross.

BOY (*loudly*). When my father's cross, he says . . .

WOMAN (*hastily*). Yes, never mind. Shall I start the story ?

CHILDREN. Yes !

SECOND GIRL. What's it called ?

WOMAN. It's called *A Christmas Carol.*

3

EFFECTS CUE : (*Soft carol music is heard off stage*).

(*She reads.*) " Marley was dead, to begin with. There is no doubt whatever about that. The register of burial was signed by the clergyman, the clerk, the undertaker and the chief mourner. Scrooge signed it. And Scrooge's name was good for anything he chose to put it to.

Old Marley was dead as a doornail. Did Scrooge know he was dead ? Of course he did. How could it be otherwise ? Scrooge and he were partners for I don't know how many years. The firm was known as Scrooge and Marley. Sometimes people new to the business called Scrooge Scrooge and sometimes Marley, but he answered to both names. It was all the same to him.

Oh, but he was a tight-fisted hand at the grindstone, Scrooge . . ."

ACT I

SCENE.—SCROOGE's office. *This is painted a dark green colour, and has dusty mahogany furniture and a threadbare carpet on the floor. Down* L. *is a large hooded fireplace, with a mantelshelf on which stand an unlit candle in a candlestick, a black marble clock, a pewter mug containing quill pens and a mass of account books and papers. A small fire burns in the grate between iron fire-dogs. The hearth contains fire-irons, a brass scuttle of coal and a pewter mug with tapers. A wing armchair stands at the top end of the fireplace. Up* L. *a heavy cabinet contains ledgers, account-books, six bags of coins, a large cash-box full of loose coins, a bottle of sherry and two glasses. A portrait of* MARLEY *hangs on the wall up* C., *and between this and the window, which is furnished with a dark blue pelmet and curtains, a brass bell juts out from the cornice. The door to the outer office is down* R., *with an upper glass panel inscribed "*SCROOGE AND MARLEY.*" Up stage of the door there is a ' blind break ' in the side wall to allow for the entrance of* MARLEY's GHOST *under cover of the opened door. A flat desk stands* C. *On it are a pen tray, a quill pen in an inkpot, an unlit candle in a candlestick, ledgers and papers, an open account book and a small cash-box. An upright mahogany chair stands at either side of the desk. There is another upright chair between the window and* MARLEY's *portrait.*

(*See the Ground Plan at the end of the Play.*)

The TRAVERSE CURTAIN *opens.*

LIGHTING CUE. A spotlight fades in on SCROOGE.

He stands behind his desk and counts money into the cash-box. The WOMAN *continues reading.*

" A squeezing, wrenching, grasping, scraping, covetous old sinner.

(SCROOGE *chuckles over the money.*)

Hard and sharp as flint, secret and self-contained, solitary as an oyster.

5

(SCROOGE *rises and crosses to the fire to warm his hands.*)

The cold within him froze his old features, nipped his pointed nose—(SCROOGE *rubs his nose.*)—shrivelled his cheek—(SCROOGE *walks stiffly back to his desk.*)—and stiffened his gait, and spoke out shrewdly in his grating voice.

(SCROOGE *chuckles throatily and sits at the desk.*)

But what did he care ? Well, once upon a time, on, of all the good days in the year, Christmas Eve, old Scrooge sat busy in his chambers adjoining his office. It was cold, bleak, biting weather and foggy withal. There he sat, counting his money—

LIGHTING CUE : The lights begin to fade on the WOMAN *and* CHILDREN.

—counting his money—on Christmas Eve."

LIGHTING CUE : The lights fade out completely down R.

(*The* WOMAN *and* CHILDREN *lift the armchair and go off through* R. *arch.*)

LIGHTING CUE : The lights come up fully in SCROOGE's *office. It is late afternoon and a yellow foggy light can be seen outside the window.* SCROOGE *counts the last of the coins into his cash-box, and bends to enter the total in his account-book.*)

SCROOGE (*writing*). That makes ten pounds, eight shillings, one penny and three farthings.

(*There is a knock at the door.* BOB CRATCHIT *enters and stands hesitating inside the door. He is a poorly-dressed, kindly man of middle-age. He carries a ledger under his arm.*)

SCROOGE (*looking up*). Yes ? Yes ? What is it ? What d'you want ?
BOB. If you please, sir . . .
SCROOGE. Well ?
BOB. I came in to . . .
SCROOGE (*finally*). No, you can't.
BOB. Can't what, sir ?
SCROOGE. You can't have any more coal for the fire. D'you think I'm made of coal ?

Bob. No, sir, but . . .

Scrooge (*warming up*). Mr. Cratchit, have you considered the monstrous price these scoundrels are asking for a miserable hundredweight of coal ? Ruinous ! Ruinous, Cratchit We shall all be in the poor house if we don't take care, all of us.

Bob. Yes, sir, but, it wasn't . . .

Scrooge (*rising*). Not another word, Cratchit, or I shall be obliged to find myself another clerk. God bless my soul, if it wasn't Christmas Eve, I should order you off my premises for good.

Bob. I'm sorry, sir.

Scrooge. Sorry, sir ! Does " Sorry, sir " replace the guineas you burn away in there every week ? I'm afraid I've been too kind to you, Cratchit. Too kind. (*He indicates the account book that* Cratchit *holds.*) What's that you've got ?

Bob. The weekly account, sir.

Scrooge. Well, well, let me have it.

(Cratchit *crosses to the desk and gives the book to* Scrooge. Scrooge *sits behind the desk and runs his finger down the columns.*)

Scrooge. Hmm ! Hmm ! (*He finds a huge profit figure and is delighted.*) Hmmm ! (*Suddenly he frowns.*) Mr. Cratchit, what's this ?

Bob (*nervously*). What, sir ? (*He cranes over the desk to look at the ledger.*)

Scrooge (*ominously calm.*) When you first came here, Cratchit, you assured me, with every appearance of honesty, that you were familiar with the principles of arithmetic.

Bob. I am, sir.

Scrooge. Then, sir, pray add the following. (*He reads rapidly.*) " One pound four shillings two pence and one halfpenny *plus* seventeen shillings and eightpence."

Bob (*adding desperately*). Two pounds, one shilling and tenpence halfpenny, sir.

Scrooge (*most amiably*). Correct, Mr. Cratchit. My congratulations.

Bob (*flustered*). Thank you, sir.

Scrooge (*suddenly roaring*). Then why, Cratchit, is the very same sum entered in this book as " Two pounds one shilling and ten pence." (*Menacingly*.) Where is the missing halfpenny ?

(CRATCHIT *is silent*.)

Well ?

BOB (*miserably*). I'm very sorry, sir. I must have made a mistake.

SCROOGE. A very grave one, Cratchit. I had always considered your bookkeeping to be most satisfactory. (*He corrects himself*.) Well, fairly satisfactory. But I see that I was mistaken.

BOB (*indicating the portrait*). Mr. Marley, sir, was good enough to say that my books were the finest he had ever . . .

SCROOGE (*snarling*). Marley's dead. Dead as a doornail. Has been for seven years.

BOB (*warmly*). Yes, sir, but *when* he was alive . . .

SCROOGE. Does Mr. Marley pay your wages every week ?

BOB. No, sir.

SCROOGE. Who does ?

BOB. You do, sir.

SCROOGE. Exactly. Then never mind Mr. Marley and his high opinion of you. (*He taps the ledger*.) What explanation have you for this ?

BOB. It wouldn't have happened any other time, sir. It's just that tonight I wanted to finish the accounts quickly and go home.

LIGHTING CUE : The lights begin to fade down slowly.

SCROOGE. And why tonight of all nights, pray ?

BOB. It's Christmas Eve, sir.

SCROOGE. I'm aware of that.

BOB. My wife and children were hoping that . . .

SCROOGE. Your wife and children are no concern of mine. Have I a wife ?

(CRATCHIT *is silent*.)

Answer me, sir, have I a wife ?

BOB. No, sir.

SCROOGE. Have I any children ?

BOB. No, sir.

SCROOGE. Do *I* want to go home ?

BOB. You *are* home, sir. You live here.

SCROOGE. That's beside the point. Well, Cratchit, as you have apparently no explanation to offer for this unparalleled error in arithmetic, you will be good enough to take this book and make a fresh account before you leave tonight. And a correct one, sir. (*He throws the book across the room.*)

BOB (*catching the ledger*).   Tonight, sir !

SCROOGE.   Tonight. And let us have no more missing halfpennies, or you'll be spending more time with your wife and children than you'll find profitable. Now go.

BOB. But—but Mrs. Cratchit will have my meal waiting, sir.

SCROOGE.   Get back to your work. (*He peers at some papers on the desk.*)

BOB. Yes, sir. (*He goes to the door, turns and says quietly.*)   You cantankerous old sinner !

SCROOGE (*lifting his head, not sure what he heard*).   What ?

BOB (*hastily*).   I said " Thank goodness it's a cold dinner," sir.

(BOB *goes out hurriedly.* SCROOGE *rises, mutters to himself and goes to the cupboard up* L. *to fetch a bottle of sherry and a glass. He brings these to the desk, then goes to the fireplace, picks up a spill and lights it. He lights the candle on the mantelshelf, and crosses to the desk and lights the candle there.*)

LIGHTING CUE :   Bring up candlelight.

SCROOGE *picks up the bottle and pours a small amount into the glass. He holds it up to the light, shakes his head and pours half of it back into the bottle.* FRED, SCROOGE'S *nephew, enters down* R. *and stands watching his uncle. He is a gaily-dressed, handsome young man, full of good humour and kindness.* SCROOGE *crosses to the fireplace and lifts his glass slowly to drink.* FRED *moves quickly and quietly towards him, and slaps him on the back.* SCROOGE *splutters wildly and spills the sherry into the hearth.*)

FRED.   A Merry Christmas, Uncle. God save you !

SCROOGE.   Damn you, nephew. Couldn't you see that I was drinking ?

FRED (*grinning*).   So you were. (*He crosses to the desk and takes the bottle.*)   Well, well, celebrating the festive occasion, eh ?   I'll join you. (*He lifts a tumbler from the desk and pours out some sherry.*)

SCROOGE (*still choking*). No ! No !

FRED (*misunderstanding deliberately*). What, not enough ? Thanks, I would like a little more. (*He fills the glass.*) To Christmas, Uncle. (*He drinks.*)

SCROOGE (*groaning*). That sherry cost me a great deal of money.

FRED. It was worth it. (*He holds out the bottle.*) Have another glass ?

SCROOGE (*snatching the bottle.*) No. (*He strokes the bottle sadly and puts it on the mantelpiece.*)

FRED (*moving to the chair* R. *of desk*). Well, Uncle, it's good to see you looking so well and happy. (*He sits and puts his feet on the desk.*) The softening effects of Christmas Eve, I suppose.

SCROOGE. Bah ! Humbug !

FRED. Christmas a humbug ! You don't mean that, surely.

SCROOGE. I do. " Merry Christmas " indeed. What right have you got to be merry ? You're poor enough.

FRED (*taking out a cigar from his pocket*). Pooh ! What's money ?

SCROOGE (*astounded*). What's money ?

FRED. Oh, come on, Uncle. What right have you got to be dismal ? You're rich enough. (*He stretches for the candle.*)

SCROOGE. Bah !

FRED (*lighting his cigar*). Now don't be cross, Uncle.

SCROOGE. I will be cross. What else can I be when I live in such a world of fools as this ? What's Christmas to you but a time of paying bills ?

FRED. And getting presents.

SCROOGE. And finding yourself a year older and not an hour richer ?

FRED. But much wiser—and happier.

SCROOGE (*crossing to the desk*). If I had my way every idiot that goes about with " Merry Christmas " on his lips should be boiled in his own pudding and buried with a stake of holly through his heart.

FRED. But, Uncle . . .

SCROOGE (*swinging* FRED'S *legs off his desk*). Nephew, you keep Christmas in your way, and leave me to keep it in mine.

FRED. But you don't keep it.

SCROOGE. So much the better. What good has it ever done you ? What profit is there in it ?

FRED (*rising and walking up stage to the window*). If you mean money, none. But most of the good things I've had in life have given me no profit, Christmas included.

(BOB CRATCHIT *enters quietly down* R. *and stands listening.*)

But I've always thought of Christmas time as a *good* time ; a kind, charitable, forgiving sort of time. The only time I know of, in the whole of the year, when men and women seem to open up their hearts, freely and without condition. Yes, and to think of those below them not as if they were a race apart bound on other journeys, but as fellow passengers through life. (*He pauses.*) Oh, you're quite right, Uncle, Christmas has never put gold or silver in my pocket. But it's done me good before, and it'll do me good again. And I say, God bless it !

CRATCHIT (*quietly*). God bless it !

(SCROOGE *notices him.*)

SCROOGE (*snarling*). Another word from you, sir, and you lose your situation. What do you want ?

CRATCHIT. There are two gentlemen to see you, sir.

SCROOGE (*keenly*). *Business* gentlemen ?

CRATCHIT. I don't think so, sir. They were very civil.

(FRED *laughs.*)

SCROOGE. Eh ? Tell them I'll see them in a minute. (*He busies himself with the books on his desk.*)

(FRED *moves down to* CRATCHIT *and shakes hands with him.*)

FRED. How are you, Cratchit ?

CRATCHIT. Oh, I'm very well, sir, thank you.

FRED. And your wife and children ?

CRATCHIT. Well, too, sir.

FRED (*fumbling in his pocket*). I—er—I meant to get that youngest boy of yours a present, but I didn't find the time. (*He offers him some money.*) Perhaps you'll . . .

CRATCHIT (*quietly*). Thank you, sir, and no offence, but—we do well enough, sir. It's not that I don't appreciate it.

(SCROOGE *watches them out of the corner of his eye.*)

FRED (*after a pause, pocketing the money*). I understand. Well, a Merry Christmas to you all !

B

SCROOGE.   " Merry Christmas ! " If I hear those words mentioned again, I shall open my office tomorrow to make up for this waste of time. Get on with your work, Cratchit.

CRATCHIT. Yes, sir. (*He goes to the door, opens it, turns back and whispers.*) Merry Christmas !

(*He goes out.*)

SCROOGE (*sourly*).   You're free enough with your money, I see, for a man that hasn't a penny piece.

FRED (*crossing to* R. *of desk*).   Now, don't be angry, Uncle. I tell you what ! Come and have dinner with us tomorrow.

SCROOGE.   I'll see you in . . . Go to the devil, sir !

FRED (*soothingly*).   All in good time, Uncle. Then just come round for a glass of wine and a biscuit. My wife will be . . .

SCROOGE (*finding a new grievance*).   Ah, your wife ! And why did you ever get married at all ?

FRED.   Why ? Because I fell in love.

SCROOGE.   Fell in love ! What a reason ! (*He moves to the fire.*) Good afternoon.

FRED (*determined to do his best*).   Now, Uncle, you never came to see me *before* I was married. Why give it as a reason for not coming now ?

SCROOGE (*turning his back on him*).   Good afternoon !

FRED.   I want nothing from you. I ask nothing. Why can't we be friends ?

SCROOGE.   Good afternoon !

FRED (*giving it up*).   Well, I'm sorry with all my heart to find you so unreasonable. (*He crosses to the door.*) However, I made up my mind to ask you, if only because it was Christmas, and you're not going to make me lose my temper. So, a *MERRY CHRISTMAS*, Uncle. (*He exits down* R.)

SCROOGE (*swinging round*).   *GOOD AFTERNOON !*

FRED (*popping his head back through the door*).   *And* a Happy New Year !

(SCROOGE *roars at him.*)

(FRED *goes out again, banging the door.* SCROOGE, *mutters, goes to the cupboard and gets a tin box of loose money and some bags of money. He brings them to the desk.   There is a knock at the door.* SCROOGE *instinctively grasps up the money in his arms.*)

SCROOGE. Who's that ?

CRATCHIT (*entering*).   Me, sir.

SCROOGE. Yes, what is it ?

CRATCHIT. Do you wish to see the two gentlemen now, sir ?

SCROOGE. Oh, yes, send 'em in.

(CRATCHIT *turns towards the door.*)

No, wait a minute !

(CRATCHIT *stops and waits.* SCROOGE *takes the sherry bottle from the mantelpiece and goes to the cupboard to hide it. He returns to his desk.*)

I'll see them now.

CRATCHIT (*going to the door and calling*). In here, gentlemen !

(SCROOGE *sits at the desk.* TWO PORTLY GENTLEMEN *enter down* R. *They look alike, and each has a bald head, gold spectacles and a benevolent expression. They resemble two Mr. Pickwicks. Each carries a hat in his hand. They advance sedately to* C.)

1ST PORT. GENT.   Thank you.

(CRATCHIT *exits.*)

Scrooge and Marley's, I believe. Have I the pleasure of addressing Mr. Scrooge or Mr. Marley ?

SCROOGE (*ungraciously*). Mr. Marley's dead. Died seven years ago, to this very night.

1ST PORT. GENT. I see. Very sad.

SCROOGE (*indicating the portrait*). That's him. Dead as a doornail, though.

2ND PORT. GENT. Well, we have no doubt that his liberality is well represented by his surviving partner. (*He produces some papers from his overcoat pocket.*) My credentials.

1ST PORT. GENT. (*producing his own papers*). And mine, sir. (*He hands both papers to* SCROOGE.) Er—may we be seated, sir ?

SCROOGE (*examining the papers*). I suppose so.

(*The* FIRST PORTLY GENTLEMAN *sits in the chair* R. *of the desk. The* SECOND PORTLY GENTLEMAN *brings the chair from up* R., *places it by the* FIRST PORTLY GENTLEMAN'S *chair and sits. Their actions are for the most part done in unison.*)

SCROOGE (*very surly*). Well ?

2ND PORT. GENT. (*coughing*). Well . . .

1ST PORT. GENT. (*coughing*). Well . . .

2ND PORT. GENT. (*taking the plunge*). Each year we consider it an honour to make the round of such gentleman as yourself in the —er—

1ST PORT. GENT. (*taking over*). In the certain knowledge that our journey will not be in vain. (*He produces a list.*) Today we have visited Pootleberry and Squib . . .

2ND PORT. GENT. (*reading from his list*). Anderson, Henderson, Sanderson, Richardson . . .

1ST PORT. GENT. And *Son*. Also Tupkins and Lovelace . . .

2ND PORT. GENT. Smith, Smith, Smith and Smith.

1ST PORT. GENT. Mr. *Smith* was most generous.

SCROOGE (*after a slight pause*). I see. You're collecting for charity.

1ST PORT. GENT. (*embarrassed*). Well, one *might* put it like that.

2ND PORT. GENT. Yes, one *might*.

SCROOGE (*playing with them*). And what did these gentlemen consider an adequate answer to your importunities ?

1ST PORT. GENT. (*rising and passing his list to* SCROOGE). I have the list here. It will be published, of course, so there is no harm in your seeing it.

2ND PORT. GENT. No, no, none at all.

1ST PORT. GENT. (*pointing out an item on the list, and excusing it*). Mr. Tupkins had no change.

2ND PORT. GENT. (*seriously*). And fourteen children.

SCROOGE (*considering the list*). Hmm ! On the whole, a very profitable excursion, if I may say so.

1ST PORT. GENT. (*sitting, rubbing his hands*). You may, Mr. Scrooge, you may.

SCROOGE (*putting a bag of money in the tin box*). Especially as money is not easily come by these days. Business is not good, gentlemen. (*He puts some more bags away.*) I will go further, gentlemen, business is *bad* ! (*He puts another bag away.*) Very bad ! (*He puts the last bag away.*)

1ST PORT. GENT. (*watching the last bag disappear*). Quite. But we thought—well, several of the gentlemen we have already visited mentioned that *you* have had a *good* year.

2ND PORT. GENT. A particularly good year.

SCROOGE (*snapping*). They were mistaken. I shall be lucky if I see a penny profit. (*He bangs the lid of the box shut.*) Bills have to be paid, sir, there's no denying them.

1ST PORT. GENT. (*warmly*). Mr. Scrooge, I feel impelled to point out that however bad a year you may, or may not, have had, there are others who have fared worse. At this season of the year, it is most desirable that we should make some provision for the poor and destitute.

2ND PORT. GENT. Many thousands lack even the bare necessities. Hundreds of thousands are without the smallest of common comforts.

SCROOGE (*rising*). Are there no prisons ?

(*The* GENTLEMEN *exchange glances.*)

1ST PORT. GENT. (*after a pause*). Plenty of prisons.

SCROOGE. And the workhouses ? Are they still in operation ?

2ND PORT. GENT. They are. I could wish they were not.

SCROOGE. The treadmill and the Poor Laws are still in good working order, I hope ?

1ST PORT. GENT. Both very busy, sir.

SCROOGE (*pleased*). Ah ! I was afraid, from what you said at first, that something had happened to stop them. Hmm ! I'm relieved to hear it.

2ND PORT. GENT. (*making a great effort*). Mr. Scrooge, a few of us are endeavouring to raise a fund to buy the poor meat and drink and means of warmth for this Christmas.

1ST PORT. GENT. We choose this time because it is, on the one hand, a time when want is keenly felt and on the other, a time when good things are in abundance. (*He picks up the list which* SCROOGE *has left on the desk.*) Now sir what shall we put you down for ?

SCROOGE (*after a slight pause*). Nothing.

1ST PORT. GENT. Oh you wish to remain anonymous ?

SCROOGE. I wish to be left alone. I don't make any extra money at Christmas and I can't afford to give it to idle people. Those who are badly off must go to the workhouse or the prisons.

1st Port. Gent.   Many *can't* go there.

2nd Port. Gent.   And many would rather die first.

Scrooge.   Then let them die and decrease the surplus population.   It's none of my business.

1st Port. Gent.   Charity is everyone's business.

Scrooge (*moving away to the fire*).   Humbug ! (*He takes some papers from the mantelpiece and studies them.*)

1st Port. Gent. (*rising*).   Really, sir, I must protest . . .

2nd Port. Gent. (*rising and returning his chair to up* R.).   Come sir.   I'm afraid we can hope for nothing here. (*He goes to the door.*)

1st Port. Gent. (*highly indignant*).   I hope, Mr. Scrooge, that you never find yourself dependent on the charity of others.   You would not find it pleasant, sir. (*He moves to the door.*)

Scrooge (*busy with papers*).   I have nothing further to say to you, gentlemen.

1st Port. Gent. (*turning from the door*).   You are the first person to refuse me charity today.   You are to be congratulated.

(*They both go out through the door in high indignation.*)

Scrooge (*snorting*).   Christmas !

(*Some carol singers begin singing " God rest you merry, Gentlemen " in the street outside.   Scrooge goes angrily to the window and shouts.*)

Here ! You !

(*The carol stops.*)

Little Boy (*off*).   Penny for the carols, sir.   Give us a penny, guv'nor !

Scrooge (*snarling*).   Be off with you !   Be off, d'you hear ?   Or I'll call the constable.

Little Boy (*off*).   Ah, yer old skinflint !

(*The carol singers hoot with derision.   They begin singing the carol again, and are heard fading away in the distance.*)

LIGHTING CUE :   The lights outside the window fade out completely, and the room is lit only by patches of light from the candles.   Scrooge mutters, crosses to the desk and puts down the papers he carries.   He picks up the tin cash-box

and goes up L. *to put it away in the cupboard.* CRATCHIT
knocks and enters down R. *with the ledger.*)

CRATCHIT. I've finished the weekly account, sir.

SCROOGE (*moving to his desk and sitting*). Let me see it.

CRATCHIT (*crossing to the top of the desk*). Yes, sir.
(*He hands the book to* SCROOGE.)

SCROOGE (*studying the book*). Hmm! Hmm! (*He looks
eagerly for a mistake. His finger rushes up and down
the columns, adding hard.*) Is that a one or a seven?

CRATCHIT (*bending over the desk to look at the book.*) A
seven, sir.

SCROOGE (*pleased*). Good! (*Darkly.*) Take more care,
Cratchit, I should hate to have to ask you to do it a third
time, eh? Eh? (*He chuckles nastily.*) Well, what are
you waiting for?

CRATCHIT. May I go now, sir?

SCROOGE. I suppose so.

CRATCHIT (*going towards the door*). Good night, sir.

SCROOGE (*stopping him*). Here, Cratchit!

CRATCHIT (*turning back*). Sir?

SCROOGE. You'll want all day off tomorrow, I suppose?

CRATCHIT (*feebly*). If it's convenient, sir.

SCROOGE (*rising, angrily*). It's *not* convenient. And it's
not fair. Why should I be put to this inconvenience every
three hundred and sixty-five days? If I were to stop half-
a-crown out of your wages, you'd think yourself ill-used,
I'll be bound.

CRATCHIT (*miserably*). Well, sir . . .

SCROOGE. And yet you don't think *me* ill-used when I
pay you a day's wages for no work.

CRATCHIT. It's only once a year, sir.

SCROOGE. A poor excuse for picking my pocket every
twenty-fifth of December. Well, I suppose you'll have to
have it. (*Sharply.*) But be here all the earlier the next
morning.

CRATCHIT. Thank you, sir. (*He goes to the door and
opens it.*) Good night, sir.

(SCROOGE *grunts.*)

And a Merry—

SCROOGE (*fiercely*). Uh?

CRATCHIT. Nothing, sir. Good night.

SCROOGE (*stopping him again*).   Cratchit ! (*He picks up the ledger from the desk.*)

CRATCHIT (*turning back, alarmed*).   Yes, sir ?

SCROOGE (*tapping the account book*).   You're sure this is a seven and not a one ?

CRATCHIT.   Certain, sir.

SCROOGE (*chuckling*).   Good. Very good. Seven pounds are better than one, Cratchit. Remember that.

CRATCHIT (*bitterly*).   I'll remember it, sir.

(*He goes out down* R. SCROOGE *takes another look at the ledger, closes it and goes up* L. *to the cupboard.*)

SCROOGE (*muttering*).   A seven and not a one. (*He notices the portrait up* C.) Doesn't make much difference to you, old Marley, does it ? It's all one to you. (*He chuckles and puts the ledger in the cupboard, then moves down to the desk and mutters.*) Candles. Cost money ! (*He blows out the candle on the desk, moves to the fireplace and blows out the candle on the mantelshelf.*)

LIGHTING CUE : Take out candlelight. The room is now lit only by firelight, which strikes across the wing armchair and on to the portrait of MARLEY *up* C.)

EFFECTS CUE : The wind begins to rise in fitful gusts.

(SCROOGE *sits in the wing armchair and mutters.*) Old Marley, eh ? Dead as a doornail. (*He yawns.*) Dead as a—(*he turns and stares at the portrait, then rises slowly and moves up* C. *to examine it more closely*)—as a doornail. (*He turns away from the portrait.*) Humbug! (*He walks back towards the fire, but turns again to peer at the portrait.*)

EFFECTS CUE : The wind howls louder.

(*The door down* R. *suddenly flies open.*)

Eh ? What ? What ? (*He hurries across the room and shuts the door. He moves back to* L. *of the desk.*)

EFFECTS CUE : The bell on the wall begins to toll slowly and gets louder and louder.

(SCROOGE *turns and watches the bell with fascination. He backs away from it towards the fireplace.*)

EFFECTS CUE : The bell stops ringing, the wind howls again, and the door crashes open.

(SCROOGE *runs across the stage to shut it.*)

(MARLEY'S GHOST *enters through the ' blind break ' in the*

wall behind the open door and stands motionless.)

(SCROOGE *closes the door and returns to* C.)

EFFECTS CUE : *There is a loud prolonged crash of music and wind.*

LIGHTING CUE : *A green spot comes up on* MARLEY'S GHOST.

(MARLEY *is dressed in olive green clothes of a period ten years earlier than that of the play. His hands and his face are green, his hair silver. A long chain, to which are fastened ledgers, cash-boxes and account books, is wrapped round his body and hands.)*

EFFECTS CUE : *The wind and the music die away.*

(SCROOGE *turns and sees* MARLEY'S GHOST. *He falls to his knees.)*

SCROOGE (*screaming*). Aaah ! (*He gathers his courage.*) What—what do you want with me ?

MARLEY (*in an evil, rasping voice*). Much.

SCROOGE. Who are you ?

MARLEY. Rather ask me who I *was* ?

SCROOGE. Who *were* you then ?

MARLEY (*advancing on him*). In life, I was your partner, Jacob Marley.

SCROOGE (*rising and backing away from* MARLEY). Yes— yes, that's it. You're Jacob Marley.

MARLEY. I *was* Jacob Marley.

SCROOGE. Well—er—will you, or rather, *can* you sit down ?

MARLEY. I can.

SCROOGE. Do so then.

MARLEY (*moving to the chair* R. *of the desk*). I see you don't believe in me. (*He sits.*)

SCROOGE (*decidedly*). I don't.

MARLEY (*snarling*). What proof of my reality would you have beyond that of your own senses ?

SCROOGE. I want no proof.

MARLEY. Then you doubt your own senses, your sight, your hearing ? Why ?

SCROOGE. Because the slightest little things may affect them. One bit of undigested beef in my stomach, together with a blot of mustard, a crumb of cheese, a bit of under-done potato, and I might see *anything*. (*He sniggers feebly*.) There's more gravy than grave about you, whatever you are.

MARLEY (*rising, smoothly and menacingly*). You were never one for making jokes, Ebeneezer. You're laughing now because you're frightened.

SCROOGE. I'm not.

MARLEY (*taking a step towards him*). You're almost paralysed with terror.

SCROOGE (*defiantly*). No.

(MARLEY *turns and sits again, facing away from* SCROOGE.)

Look, do you see this—this toothpick ? (*He picks up a toothpick from the desk*.)

MARLEY (*not looking*). I do.

SCROOGE (*pettishly*). You're not looking at it.

MARLEY. Nevertheless, I see it !

SCROOGE. Well, if I swallow it, my stomach will make me see something twice as horrible as you are in ten minutes. Humbug, I say ! Humbug ! (*He laughs non-chalantly*.)

(MARLEY *rises and faces* SCROOGE.)

MARLEY (*with a terrible cry*). Aaaah !

(SCROOGE *stops laughing and falls on his knees*.)

SCROOGE. No, no ! Mercy ! I didn't mean it. I . . .

MARLEY (*towering over him*). Do you believe in me now ?

SCROOGE (*terrified*). Yes. Yes. I must. (*He tries hard to control himself*.) But —but why have you come to me ? What do you want ?

MARLEY (*moving away to* C. *and speaking in a sepulchral voice*). It is required of every man that the Spirit within him should travel far and wide amongst his fellow men. If that Spirit does not go forth in *life*, it is condemned to do so after death—to wander abroad through the world, witnessing what it cannot share, but what it *might* have shared and turned to happiness whilst it was alive.

SCROOGE (*rising and whispering*). Why do you wear those chains ? Did you commit some horrible crime on earth ?

MARLEY (*lifting the chain*). I wear the chain that I forged for myself in life.

SCROOGE. For yourself ?

MARLEY (*sighing*). Yes. Link by link. Yard by yard, I made it. Of my own free will, I put it on. Of my own free will, I wear it ! (*Suddenly he turns and thrusts the chain towards* SCROOGE *and snarls.*) Is not the pattern familiar to you ?

SCROOGE (*shaking*). No !

MARLEY. It should be ! At this moment, at every moment of the life behind you, *you* have been forging such a chain for yourself.

SCROOGE. No. I have done nothing.

MARLEY. You have done much. (*He holds out the chain.*) Seven years ago your chain was as long and as heavy as this. Not one minute of the day has passed since then, but you have added to the horrible burden you must drag through the life after death. Yours is a ponderous chain, Ebeneezer.

(SCROOGE *looks behind himself for signs of a chain.*)

Oh, you can't see it. But it's there, Scrooge, it's there !

SCROOGE (*kneeling*). Jacob ! Old Jacob ! Help me ! Tell me what I must do ! Give me some comfort !

MARLEY (*howling with agony*). I have none to give.

SCROOGE. You must help. (*He rises and pleads desperately.*) You were my partner, Jacob. You like me. Tell me what to do. *TELL ME !*

MARLEY. I cannot! Only a little more time is permitted to me. I cannot rest nor stay. Yet—mark this—my Spirit never walks beyond these four walls, never moves beyond the limits of this money-changing hole.

(SCROOGE *moves to the armchair and prepares to sit.*)

Many a time I've sat invisible beside you—in that very chair.

SCROOGE (*leaping up*). Have you, indeed ? (*He gathers his courage.*) Well, Jacob, you've been a bit slow about it, haven't you ?

MARLEY. Slow ?

SCROOGE. Seven years dead and still travelling.

MARLEY (*writhing in his chains in torment*). No rest. No peace. Only the incessant torture of remorse ! (*He extends a hand at* SCROOGE.) Listen, Ebeneezer ! Listen carefully, before it's too late. Live if you will for a hundred years, you will not find time to do all the good that lies within your power. Will you end your days regretting the lost opportunities, bitter in the knowledge of your wasted years. Will you do as *I* did ?

SCROOGE. You ! You were always a good business man, Jacob.

MARLEY. Charity ! Mercy ! Forbearance ! They should have been my business. I should have turned to mankind. Instead, I walked through the crowds of my fellow men with my eyes turned away. They were blind to the blessed star which led the wise men to a poor stable. (*He turns his head as if he hears something.*) My time is nearly done.

SCROOGE. Then say what you have to say and go !

MARLEY. I came to warn you, Ebeneezer.

SCROOGE. Warn me ?

MARLEY. Yes. There is still a chance that you may escape *my* fate.

SCROOGE (*cheering up*). There is ?

MARLEY (*discouragingly*). A very *small* one. And if you do escape, it'll only be by my doing.

SCROOGE (*obsequiously*). You were always a good friend, Jacob. Thank you.

MARLEY. Ebeneezer, you will be—

SCROOGE. Yes ?

MARLEY (*in a terrible voice*). —haunted !

SCROOGE (*dismally*). Oh !

MARLEY. Haunted by three spirits.

SCROOGE. Is that the chance you mentioned, Jacob ?

MARLEY. It is.

SCROOGE. Then I think I'd rather not have it.

MARLEY (*urgently*). You *must* ! Without their help, you cannot hope to avoid the path I tread. (*He begins to move backwards towards the door.*) Expect the first to-morrow night, when the bell tolls one !

SCROOGE. Couldn't I take 'em all at once, and get them over with ?

MARLEY (*unheeding*). Expect the second on the second night at the same hour, and the third on the next night on the last stroke of midnight.

SCROOGE (*dismally*). Ooh !

MARLEY (*still retreating*). Good-bye, Ebeneezer. You'll never see me again.

SCROOGE (*feebly*). Good-bye, Jacob.

MARLEY. And for your own sake, remember ! Remember what has passed between us ! Remember ! (*His voice rises to a wail.*)

EFFECTS CUE : *The wind rises to a howl, and the door crashes open.*

LIGHTING CUE : *The green spot on MARLEY'S GHOST goes out.*

(SCROOGE *runs across the stage and closes the door.* MARLEY'S GHOST *has disappeared.* SCROOGE *stands shaking for a moment, then crosses to the fire, snatches up a spill from the hearth and lights it. He lights the candle on the mantelshelf, crosses to the desk and lights the candle there.*)

LIGHTING CUE : *Bring up candlelight.*

(SCROOGE *goes up* L. *to the cupboard, takes out the bottle of sherry and a glass and brings them down to the desk. He pours himself a full glass of sherry, swallows it down and tries nervously to speak.*)

SCROOGE (*very squeakily*). Humbug !

He hurriedly pours out a second glass of sherry and lifts it to his mouth as—

the CURTAIN *falls.*

ACT II

SCENE.—*The false proscenium and side arches remain in position. About fifteen feet up stage of them a rostrum, three feet high, runs across the back of the scene. A second false proscenium, flanked by pillars, is built on this rostrum. Behind this is a cyclorama or skycloth, against which will be set the backgrounds for the ' visions'. The colour of the second false proscenium and the rostrum matches that of the side-flats that run from the rostrum to the edges of the first false proscenium : all are painted a misty blue-green that can suggest both exteriors and interiors. There are large rounded arches in the side-flats at* R.C. *and* L.C.

(*See the Ground Plan at the end of the Play.*)

Before the CURTAIN *rises the carol " While Shepherds watched" is sung off stage.*

When the CURTAIN *rises the stage is in darkness. The* LIGHTS *fade in as the carol ends. The* TRAVERSE CURTAIN *is closed. Down* R. *a small bed is set facing the footlights, with a tall canopy of red brocade at its head. A small table stands* L. *of the bed ; on it are an extinguished candle in a candlestick and a watch.* SCROOGE *lies in bed ; asleep, wearing a long nightgown and a nightcap. He is snoring. A louder snore than usual wakes him and he sits up.*

SCROOGE (*startled*). What's the time ? (*He picks up his watch from the table and looks at it.*) Nearly one. (*He puts down the watch and begins to lie down again. Suddenly he remembers and sits up quickly.*) Nearly one! It's impossible! I can't have slept through a whole day and half the night. (*He takes the watch from the table.*) There must be an icicle in the works. (*He shakes it.*) Must be wrong ! Can't be one o'clock. (*He settles down in bed again.*)

EFFECTS CUE : A church clock begins chiming the quarters.

(SCROOGE *sits up in bed again.*)

24

(*Counting the chimes.*)   Quarter ! Half ! Three-quarters !
The hour ! (*With great relief.*) And nothing else !

EFFECTS CUE :   The clock chimes One.

*LIGHTING CUE :   A flash-box is fired in the footlights.
    Bring up pink following spot on the* SPIRIT.

(THE SPIRIT OF CHRISTMAS PAST *puts its face through the
    canopy at the head of the bed. It wears a full-length pale
    grey robe. Its face is young but its hair is silver and is
    swept up to a light that burns on its head. The* SPIRIT
    *carries a large candle extinguisher in its hand. It speaks
    with a young voice.* SCROOGE *scrambles to the foot of the
    bed in terror.*)

SCROOGE (*after a pause*).   Are—are you the Spirit whose
coming was foretold to me ?

CH. PAST.   I am.

SCROOGE.   Who and what are you ?

CH. PAST.   I am the Spirit of Christmas Past !

SCROOGE (*quavering*).   Long past ?

CH. PAST.   *Your* past.

SCROOGE.   Oh. Well—er—(*He looks at the light burning
on the* SPIRIT's *head.*)—pray take off your cap, sir, it must
be uncomfortable. And you might set fire to the bed.

CH. PAST (*sternly*).   Would you put out the light I give
so soon ? Isn't it enough that you and your passions have
made this cap ?

SCROOGE.   Made it ?

CH. PAST.   Aye, and forced me to wear it through the
unending years.

(*The* SPIRIT's *head disappears through the canopy.* SCROOGE
    breathes a sigh of relief. The SPIRIT *re-appears* L. *of the
    bed.*)

SCROOGE (*beginning immediately to protest*).   Oh, but I
didn't. I assure you, most humbly, I had nothing whatever
to do with it. (*He fawns*). Dear kind Spirit, what brings
you here ?

CH. PAST.   Your welfare.

SCROOGE.   Please, I'd much rather have a good night's
rest.

CH. PAST.   Your reclamation then. (*He takes one step
back.*) Come with me !

SCROOGE. Really, it's very cold and I'm sure . . .

CH. PAST. Come !

SCROOGE (*whining*). But this bed's so warm. It seems such a pity.

(*The* SPIRIT *takes no notice.*)

But I've only got a nightgown on, and it's freezing. I've got the most dreadful cold. Listen. (*He coughs and sneezes most unconvincingly.*)

CH. PAST (*commanding*). Come !

SCROOGE (*almost weeping*). All right. I'm coming. (*He gets out of bed.*)

LIGHTING CUE : Take out the light on the bed.

(*The* TRAVERSE CURTAIN *opens, revealing a dark inner stage. The rostrum at the back is lit with the deep gold rays of the setting sun. Behind it there is a line of snow-covered hills and trees, against a sky red with winter sunset.* SCROOGE *moves up* R. *and mounts the steps to stand on the rostrum. The* SPIRIT OF CHRISTMAS PAST *follows him and climbs to the top step, where it stands.*)

SCROOGE (*looking round in amazement*). Good Heavens ! This is the place where I was born. I was a boy here !

CH. PAST. Your lips are trembling. (*It points with the extinguisher.*) And what's that on your cheek ?

SCROOGE (*gruffy*). Nothing ! Nothing ! It's a pimple. (*He is crying.*)

CH. PAST. It's a very wet one.

SCROOGE. Humbug !

CH. PAST. Do you remember this lane ?

SCROOGE. Remember it ? I could walk it blindfold.

CH. PAST (*quietly*). Then it's strange that you've forgotten it for so many years.

SCROOGE (*looking off* L.). There are some people coming. (*He hurries back to the top of the steps.*)

CH. PAST. Oh, they can't see us. They're only the shadow of things that have been in the past.

(DANIEL, *an old farm-labourer, wearing a smock, enters from* L. *of the rostrum to* C. *of the rostrum, and stands to look at the view.*)

SCROOGE (*astonished*). Why, it's old Daniel Whetstone ! He used to dance me on his knee.

(FARMER *and* MRS. GREENROW *follow* DANIEL *on to the rostrum. They are dressed in clothes of a generation earlier than the period of the play.*)

And there's Farmer Greenrow and his good wife. They gave me apples.

DANIEL (*touching his hat*). A Merry Christmas, Mrs. Greenrow. And to you, Jim.

GREENROW. And the same to you, old fellow.

(*The imaginary figures pass along to* R. *of the rostrum.*)

MRS. GREENROW (*going*). There's a mug of ale for you at the farm tonight, Daniel . . .

(*They go off* R. *on the rostrum.*)

SCROOGE (*stepping on to the rostrum and muttering*). " Merry Christmas ! " What good did it ever do anyone ? (*He looks off stage* R.)

(*The* SPIRIT *moves to* C. *of the rostrum.*)

CH. PAST (*pointing into the darkness down stage* L.). Do you remember that building ?

SCROOGE (*joining the* SPIRIT *at* C.). Aye, it's the old schoolhouse. Oh, it was a bleak place, Spirit. Be thankful you never went there. I did my sums there. I was ever a one for sums. Learn the difference between a seven and a one, Spirit, that's the way to riches.

CH. PAST (*taking no notice*). The children are on holiday now—all except one.

SCROOGE (*dimly remembering*). One ?

CH. PAST (*deliberately*). A little boy. His friends had forgotten him. He's still there, all by himself.

LIGHTING CUE : Bring up a spotlight on L.C.

(*A* SMALL BOY *sits on a tin trunk* L.C. *with his back to the audience, and his head in his hands. Painted on the trunk is* " E. SCROOGE.")

SCROOGE (*sadly*). I remember. I remember. Poor boy.

CH. PAST. You pity him ?

SCROOGE. Aye, I pity him. I wish . . .

CH. PAST. Yes ?

SCROOGE. No. It's too late now.

CH. PAST. What is ?

SCROOGE (*muttering*). Nothing. There was a boy singing a Christmas carol at my window yesterday. I should like to have given him something, that's all.

LIGHTING CUE : Fade out the spotlight on L.C.

(*The* SMALL BOY *goes out through the arch* L.C. *and takes the trunk with him.*)

CH. PAST (*smiling*). Well, shall we see another Christmas? You've had a good many in the past, you know. Or perhaps you've forgotten.
        SCROOGE. It's so long ago.
        CH. PAST. Pooh ! What an excuse ! I can remember a thousand years ago as if it was yesterday. (*The* SPIRIT *points into the darkness halfway down stage* R.C.) Do you see that door ?
        SCROOGE. Aye.
        CH. PAST. Do you recall it ?
        SCROOGE (*slowly*). Yes. It's old Fezziwig's. I was apprenticed there.

LIGHTING CUE : Bring up a spotlight R.C.

(MR. FEZZIWIG *enters through the arch* R.C. *He carries some papers. He is dressed in clothes of the period of* SCROOGE's *youth, and wears a curled powdered wig, a full red coat and an embroidered waistcoat. He has a red, jovial face and his age is about fifty.*)

And there he is ! Bless my soul ! Old Fezziwig alive again !
        CH. PAST. Listen.

(MR. FEZZIWIG *fusses about anxiously and takes out his watch.*)

FEZZIWIG (*looking at his watch*). Dear, dear ! Seven o'clock and still here. What must they think of me ? (*He calls off* R.) Dick ! Ebeneezer ! Come in here !

(DICK WILKINS, *a young clerk, runs in through the arch* R.C. *to* R. *of* MR. FEZZIWIG.)

        DICK. Yes, Mr. Fezziwig ?

(MR. FEZZIWIG *gives him some papers and calls his attention to some items on them.*)

SCROOGE (*delighted*). It's Dick Wilkins. Oh, he was very much attached to me was Dick Wilkins. (*He shakes his head.*) Poor Dick ! Poor Dick !

*LIGHTING CUE : Fade out all lights on the rostrum
                area and cyclorama.*

(SCROOGE *and* SPIRIT *go off* L. *along the rostrum.*)

MR. FEZZIWIG. Where's young Ebeneezer ?

DICK. He's taking those letters round to the Temple, sir. He'll not be long.

MR. FEZZIWIG. Never mind, never mind. When he comes back, tell him to lock up and be off. You too. Go on. Seven o'clock on Christmas Eve and still here ! Let's have the shutters up. No more tonight.

DICK (*moving towards the arch* R.C.). Yes, sir.

MR. FEZZIWIG (*stopping him*). Oh, Dick.

DICK (*turning*). Sir ?

MR. FEZZIWIG. Don't forget you and Ebeneezer are invited to my Christmas party tonight. Mrs. Fezziwig will never forgive me if you're not there.

DICK (*going off through the arch*). We'll be there, sir. Thank you.

LIGHTING CUE : Bring up forestage lights.

(MR. FEZZIWIG *mimes the whole of the following scene.*)

MR. FEZZIWIG (*fussing*). Dear, dear ! what they must think of me. I shall have to take a carriage home or Mrs. Fezziwig will be having the vapours. Now, where's my greatcoat and scarf ? (*He takes an imaginary scarf and winds it round and round his neck, then lifts down an imaginary greatcoat and puts it on. He moves to open an imaginary door, but stops because he has forgotten his hat.*) Oh, my hat ! (*He crosses the room, takes down an imaginary hat from the hat-peg and pops it on his head.*) Now then ! (*He crosses the room, opens the door, goes through it, shuts it behind him, and begins descending an imaginary spiral staircase. He gets faster and faster as he trots round and round, stumbles, almost falls but saves himself by an imaginary banister. At the bottom of the steps he opens an imaginary front door and steps downstage below the level of the traverse curtain as if into the street.*)

(*The* TRAVERSE CURTAIN *closes behind him.*)

(*Holding out his hand*). H'mm! Snowing again! (*He beats his arms against his sides for warmth, then notices some children snowballing.*) Look at the little urchins snowballing each other! (*He roars with laughter. An imaginary snowball nearly hits him.*) Hey! Careful now! You nearly hit me then! (*A snowball does hit him, and he wipes the snow from his face.*) You did hit me! (*He sees an imaginary carriage coming from down R.*) Hey! There's a carriage! Hi! Hi! (*He runs towards the carriage, which almost runs him down.*) Confound the fellow! (*He sees another carriage from down R.*) Hi! Carriage! Stop! Here! (*His eyes follow the carriage as it slowly stops.*) That's it! (*He goes round to the front of the carriage and talks to the horse.*) Ah, there's a nice horse! There's a fine fellow. Think I might have a bit of sugar here for you. Yes! There you are! (*He takes a lump of sugar from his pocket and offers it to the horse, which bites him.*) Ow! (*He opens the door of the carriage, gets in, closes the door, and puts his head through the window to talk to the driver.*) Seventeen, Church Crescent, my good fellow. (*He sits back in his seat, and begins to jolt more and more violently. He puts his head through the window and shouts angrily.*) Here, drive more slowly! Can you hear me? I'm being broken to pieces! (*Suddenly he falls on the floor as the carriage stops abruptly.*) Confound the fellow! (*He steps out of the carriage.*) It's a good thing it's Christmas. (*He takes money from his pocket and pays the driver.*) Here you are, my man. (*He takes out some more coins and offers them.*) And here! No, no! Pray don't mention it. Off you go! (*He watches the carriage as it drives away and walks towards the arch down L., but stops as he sees a slide.*) Ooh! A slide! (*He looks round to see if anyone is watching, then crosses to down R., takes a short run to C. and slithers off through the arch down L. He falls hard on his bottom as he goes through the arch and there is a tremendous crash from off stage.*)

The TRAVERSE CURTAIN *opens to reveal the* FEZZIWIG'S *drawing-room. Tall windows stand along the front of the rostrum. A low balustrade runs along the back of the rostrum, and the outline of trees, shrubs and snow-covered walls can be seen against the sky. In the room below the rostrum there is an ornate table* C., *on which are glasses and a large punch bowl. Up stage* L. *stands a small sofa. Up* R. *a screen hides the steps to the rostrum. Draped curtains hang in the arches* R.C. *and* L.C.

LIGHTING CUE : Bring up main stage lights.

(MR. FEZZIWIG *enters through the arch* L.C. MRS. FEZZIWIG *enters at the same time through the arch* R.C. *She is about fifty and is wearing her party dress.*)

MRS. FEZZIWIG (*crossing to him*). My dear, how late you are !

MR. FEZZIWIG. I'm sorry, my dear. I didn't notice the time. Here, a peace offering. (*He produces a box containing a brooch.*)

MRS. FEZZIWIG. For me ? But you've already given me seven Christmas presents.

MR. FEZZIWIG. Have I ? Well, well, can't have too many. Aren't you going to open it ?

MRS. FEZZIWIG. Of course ! (*She opens the box and looks at the brooch.*) Oh, you darling ! (*She kisses him.*)

MR. FEZZIWIG (*fussing*). Now, now, is everything ready ?

(MRS. FEZZIWIG *tries to tell him.*)

What about the punch ?

(MRS. FEZZIWIG *tries again to tell him.*)

Are you sure it's properly mixed ?

(MRS. FEZZIWIG *tries once more.*)

Have the musicians arrived ?

MRS. FEZZIWIG (*laughing*). Yes !

MR. FEZZIWIG (*crossing her to* L. *of the table*). All the same, I think I'll try the punch. (*He pours out a glass of punch and tastes it.*) A glass for you, my dear ?

MRS. FEZZIWIG. No, thank you.

MR. FEZZIWIG (*tasting the punch again*). Mmm ! Delicious !

(*There is a sound of voices and laughter off* L.)

MRS. FEZZIWIG (*beginning to panic*). There are the first guests, my dear ! (*She goes to him.*) Quickly, straighten your cravat ! (*She arranges his cravat.*) That's better ! Oh, where are the children ? They should be here. (*She crosses to* R.C.) Bless my soul, where are those girls ?

(MISS FANNY FEZZIWIG *and* MISS EMMA FEZZIWIG *enter through the* R.C. *arch. They are attractive girls of about twenty, but* EMMA *is considerably more serious than* FANNY. *They move to the* R. *of* MRS. FEZZIWIG.)

Oh, there you are ! Come and stand beside me to welcome the guests. Where's your father ?

(MR. FEZZIWIG *pours himself another glass of punch.*)

FANNY } *(together)*.   At the punch !
EMMA

MRS. FEZZIWIG (*turning to him, desperately*). My dear, the guests !

MR. FEZZIWIG (*unperturbed*). Yes, yes, my love ! At once. (*He moves round behind the table to* R. *of it.*)

MRS. FEZZIWIG. *Do* come along ! (*She crosses to* L.C. *above the arch and leads the girls with her.*) Emma, your hair ! Fanny, your dress ! (*She stops* L.C., *arranges the girls on either side of her and gives them a last quick tidy.*)

(JACOB MARLEY, *as a young man, escorts* DORA, *a very pretty girl, through the arch* L.C. *As they see their hostess, they stop.* DORA *curtsies and* JACOB *bows.* FANNY *and* EMMA *return the curtsy.*)

Dora, my dear ! And Mr. Marley ! You're the first !

MARLEY. Good evening, ma'am !

DORA. I hope we're not early.

MRS. FEZZIWIG. Of course not. You've met Emma and Fanny, have you not ?

MARLEY (*bowing again*). Of course !

(*General murmurs of* " How do you do ? ")

MRS. FEZZIWIG (*calling to* MR. FEZZIWIG). Edward ! I'm sure Mr. Marley would like some punch.

MARLEY. Mr. Marley certainly would. (*He crosses to the table.*) Good evening, Edward !

MR. FEZZIWIG. Evening to you, Jacob ! (*He shakes hands with* MARLEY, *then takes up the punch-ladle and fills two glasses.*)

MRS. FEZZIWIG (*to* DORA). Are you cold, my dear ? It's freezing out.

DORA. No, no. It's wonderfully warm in here.

MR. FEZZIWIG (*handing a glass of punch to* MARLEY). There you are, Jacob. (*He picks up his own glass.*) Merry Christmas to you !

MARLEY (*raising his glass*). And to you, Edward !

(*They drink to each other.*)

MRS. FEZZIWIG (*leading* DORA *up* L. *to the sofa*). Come
and sit down, my dear. I have the most extraordinary
thing to tell you—(*they sit*)—about Mrs. Chambers . . .

(*They continue to talk quietly.*)

FANNY (*watching* MARLEY, *and whispering to* EMMA).
Isn't he handsome ?
EMMA (*severely*).   You mustn't say that ! He's married!

(AUGUSTA *and* ADOLPHUS *enter through the* L.C. *arch.*)

Mama ! Mama ! More guests !

(EMMA *curtsies to the new arrivals. They bow and curtsy
to her.* FANNY *slips over to the table to talk to* MARLEY.
DORA *rises from the sofa and moves to the table to join*
FANNY *and* MARLEY. MRS. FEZZIWIG *rises from the sofa
and moves down stage to* R. *of* EMMA *to welcome her new
guests.*)

MRS. FEZZIWIG (*apologizing*). I'm so sorry ! (*She
curtsies.*) Augusta ! And Adolphus ! How wonderful you
could come !

(AUGUSTA *and* ADOLPHUS *curtsy and bow to her.*)

Edward was worried the snow would prevent you.
AUGUSTA.   Adolphus borrowed his father's carriage.
MRS. FEZZIWIG.   How kind of his father.
ADOLPHUS.   He doesn't know yet.
MRS. FEZZIWIG (*laughing*).   Go over and talk to Edward.
He'll be so happy to see you. (*She calls to* MR. FEZZIWIG.)
Edward, my dear, see to the punch !

(AUGUSTA *and* ADOLPHUS *cross to the table.* MR. FEZZIWIG
welcomes them and gets them glasses of punch. MARLEY,
FANNY *and* DORA *move away from the table to* R.C. *to
make room for the newcomers.*)

(*To* EMMA.) Emma, your hair is coming down again !
MR. FEZZIWIG. Ah, Adolphus, how splendid ! And
this is your new little wife, eh ? (*He takes her hand.*)
Well, well, you're a fortunate fellow.
EMMA (*whispering*).   Mama, Augusta has got powder on
her face.

MRS. FEZZIWIG. Never mind, dear, it's Christmas. We must be charitable.. (MRS. FEZZIWIG *leaves* EMMA *and crosses to the table to talk to her guests.*)

(SCROOGE, *young, gay and debonair in his party clothes, enters through the arch* L.C. *with* DICK WILKINS. EMMA *greets them.* FANNY *sees their entrance and hurries across to greet them also.*)

FANNY (*delighted*). Ebeneezer !
EMMA (*delighted*). And Dick !
FANNY. A Merry Christmas to you !
SCROOGE (*bowing*). And to you, Miss Fezziwig !
DICK (*bowing to* EMMA). Miss Fezziwig, my happiness is now complete.
MRS. FEZZIWIG (*turning from the table and seeing them*). Edward ! The boys have arrived !
MR. FEZZIWIG. Why, so they have ! (*He crosses to the* L. *of* FANNY). Come in, lads ! Ah, I see you've found my daughter's already. They've been fretting their hearts away in case you couldn't come.
EMMA (*severely*). Really, Papa !
FANNY. Don't be silly, Emma. Of course we have.
MR. FEZZIWIG. Will you take a glass of punch, Dick ?
DICK (*gazing at* EMMA). What ? Oh, no, thank you, sir.

(MARLEY *and* DORA *join* MRS. FEZZIWIG, AUGUSTA *and* ADOLPHUS *around the punch-bowl.*)

MR. FEZZIWIG. Ebeneezer, a glass for you ?
SCROOGE (*gazing at* FANNY). What ? Oh, no, thank you sir.
MR. FEZZIWIG (*at a loss*). Oh ! Well—er—I'd better leave you four to get on.

(MR. FEZZIWIG *moves away to join the party at the table.*)

EMMA (*leading* DICK *down* R.). Do you like dancing, Mr. Wilkins ?
DICK. I love it. But I'm afraid I'm a little out of practice.
FANNY (*leading* SCROOGE *down* L.). Do you like dancing, Mr. Scrooge ?
SCROOGE. I love it. But I'm afraid I'm a little out of practice.
DICK. Do you find it hot in here, Miss Fezziwig ?

EMMA. Yes, it is a little. Shall we go into the conservatory ? It's cooler in there.

DICK (*eagerly*). Of course !

SCROOGE. Do you find it cold in here, Miss Fezziwig ?

FANNY. Yes, it is a little. Shall we go into the library ? It's warmer in there.

(DICK *and* EMMA *move towards the arch down* R. *and* SCROOGE *and* FANNY *move towards the arch down* L. *They are stopped by* MR. FEZZIWIG. *He comes down* C. *and calls to them.*)

MR. FEZZIWIG. Come now, let's have the first dance. Where are the musicians ? (*He looks out front, into the orchestra pit.*) Oh, there you are ! Strike up, lads ! *Sir Roger de Coverley.*

(*The introduction to the music begins. The guests line up, men on one side, women on the other. They chatter and laugh gaily.* SCROOGE *is opposite* FANNY : DICK *is opposite* EMMA. *The* MEN *bow, the* LADIES *curtsy, and the dance begins. At the end of each figure, the couple furthest up stage makes an arch of their arms and the other four couples dance through it.*)

EFFECTS CUE : Snow begins to fall outside the windows.

(*After several turns,* SCROOGE *and* FANNY *dance first through the arch of arms. They run off hand in hand through the arch down* L. *After the next turn,* DICK *and* EMMA *are the first couple through. They run off through the arch down* R. *The other couples continue to dance several more turns until the dance reaches its climax. They laugh and call each other hilariously.*)

LIGHTING CUE : Fade quickly to blackout at the climax of the dance.

The TRAVERSE CURTAIN *closes, and the music continues softly until—*

LIGHTING CUE : Bring in spotlight on the area around the bed down R.

(SCROOGE, *wearing his cap and nightgown, runs in from the arch down* L. *to the bed. The* SPIRIT OF CHRISTMAS PAST *follows him.*)

SCROOGE (*shaken by what he has seen*). Leave me !
Leave me ! I don't want to see any more ! I don't want
to remember ! (*He turns away from the* SPIRIT *and moves
to extreme down* R.)

CH. PAST. Are you afraid ? All I have shown you is
the past.

SCROOGE. The past is gone ; let it lie dead !

CH. PAST. It will never die ; not while you live.

SCROOGE (*turning and approaching the* SPIRIT). Leave
me ! Haunt me no longer ! Go ! Go ! Go ! (*He seizes
the candle extinguisher from the* SPIRIT's *hand and forces it
on to the light on the* SPIRIT's *head.*)

LIGHTING CUE : There is a Blackout.

(*The* SPIRIT OF CHRISTMAS PAST *goes out quickly through
the arch down* L.)

*LIGHTING CUE : Bring up a faint light on the area
down* R.

(SCROOGE *is on his knees beside the bed, with his head in his
hands. He looks up cautiously, gets to his feet and clambers
into bed. He pulls the bedclothes up over his head.*)

*EFFECTS CUE : The carol " Silent Night, Holy Night "
begins softly. As it grows louder—*

*LIGHTING CUE : The lights grow brighter to indicate
the coming of morning.*

(SCROOGE *stirs uneasily in the bed.*)

*LIGHTING CUE : The lights grow to a warm afternoon
light. When the carol reaches its end they fade slowly to
night lighting.*)

*EFFECTS CUE : A church clock strikes the quarters and
one o'clock.*

(SCROOGE *wakes up.*)

SCROOGE (*quavering*). Who's there ? (*He looks cautiously
behind the canopy curtains, then bends to look under each
side of the bed and over the downstage end of it. He gets
gingerly out of bed, puts on the slippers that lie beside it,
and moves* C. *to peer into the darkness off* L.)

(*The* SPIRIT OF CHRISTMAS PRESENT *enters through the arch down* R. *He can be dressed either as in the illustrations to Dicken's story, or as a conventional Father Christmas.*)

LIGHTING CUE : *Bring up a red following spot on the* SPIRIT OF CHRISTMAS PRESENT.

(*The* SPIRIT *moves round the bottom of the bed and sits on the* L. *side of it.* SCROOGE *backs slowly towards the bed, turns round and suddenly sees the* SPIRIT. *He jumps backwards with alarm.*)

CH. PRES. (*roaring with laughter*).   Come, come, man ! You ought to know me better.

SCROOGE (*chattering his teeth*).   Are you the . . . the . . . ?

CH. PRES.   Yes, the Spirit of Christmas Present. Have you ever seen anything like me before ?

SCROOGE (*with conviction*).   Never !

CH. PRES.   Never met any of my brothers before ?

SCROOGE.   No,—brothers ! Have you got *brothers* ?

CH. PRES.   Oh, yes. Over eighteen hundred of 'em. What d'you think of that ?

SCROOGE.   I think it's a large family to provide for.

CH. PRES. (*rising*).   Well, are you ready to follow me ?

SCROOGE (*after a slight pause*).   Take me where you will. Last night I went on compulsion. I learned a lesson which is working in me now. Tonight, if you have anything to teach me, then let me profit by it.

(*The* TRAVERSE CURTAIN *opens.* SCROOGE *and the* SPIRIT OF CHRISTMAS PRESENT *move up* R. *to the steps that lead to the rostrum.*)

The rostrum now represents a street on a clear crisp winter's morning. A snow-covered pillar box stands L. *on the rostrum. A tall green lamp-post stands at the* R. *The sky is a hard steely blue, and the rostrum area is flooded with bright sunshine.*

As SCROOGE *and the* SPIRIT *reach the steps, the* FIRST COCKNEY *enters along the rostrum from* L. *He carries a cloth bag of bottles, and wears a muffler, a greatcoat and a shabby hat. A moment after he has entered, the* SECOND COCKNEY *enters along the rostrum from* R. *He carries a number of parcels and is dressed like the* FIRST COCKNEY.

They collide R.C. *of the rostrum and their parcels fall to the ground.*)

1ST COCKNEY (*glaring*). Why can't yer look where you're going ?

2ND COCKNEY. I was looking, see ? What's come ter yer eyes ? Yer walked straight into me, see ?

1ST COCKNEY (*getting more heated*). All I wanter know is " Oo's going ter pay fer my bottles ? " That's all I wanter know. Are *you* ?

2ND COCKNEY (*very heated*). Never mind your bottles. What abaht my parcels ?

1ST COCKNEY. Pick yer perishing parcels up. And mind my bottles.

2ND COCKNEY. Blast yer bottles, they ain't broke.

1ST COCKNEY. No more ain't yer parcels.

2ND COCKNEY. Orlright! Pick 'em up for me! Go on!

1ST COCKNEY. Pick 'em up, 'e says ! Yer can pick up yer own blooming parcels !

2ND COCKNEY. Oh, I can, can I ? Yer little shrimp, I'll give yer pick 'em up !

1ST COCKNEY (*squaring up*). Come on then. 'Oo's waiting ?

(*They raise their fists and spar up to each other. The* SPIRIT *steps on to the rostrum and passes quietly between them. The two* COCKNEYS *immediately drop their aggressive attitudes, stare at each other and burst out laughing.* SCROOGE *watches them fascinated from the steps.*)

2ND COCKNEY (*offering his hand*). Sorry matey. Can't 'ave this sort of thing, can we ?

1ST COCKNEY (*shaking it warmly*). Not at Christmas, no. 'Ere, let me pick up them parcels fer you. (*He stoops to pick up the parcels.*)

2ND COCKNEY. Nah, don't bother, I can find 'em. What abaht them bottles of yourn ? (*He stoops to pick up the bag of bottles.*)

1ST COCKNEY. I got 'em. (*They exchange parcels and bottles.*) 'Ere, 'ow abaht coming back wiv me and knocking a couple of 'em orf ?

2ND COCKNEY. Orlright ! I got some steak an' kidney pies 'ere ! We'll 'ave a bite out of them.

1st Cockney. Orlright. Come on, matey !

(*They link arms and disappear along the rostrum to* R.)

Scrooge (*amazed*). Did you see that ?
Ch. Pres. *See* it ? I *did* it ! (*He moves* R. *on the rostrum.*)

(Bob Cratchit *comes along the rostrum from* L. *He carries* Tiny Tim *on his shoulder.* Tiny Tim *holds a rough wooden crutch in one hand, and clasps his father's neck with the other.* Bob Cratchit *stops and points out various things of interest to* Tiny Tim *in the street.*)

Scrooge (*pointing*). Look, there's Cratchit !
Ch. Pres. Yes, Bob Cratchit. Your clerk.
Scrooge. Who's the boy on his shoulder ?
Ch. Pres. Don't you know ?
Scrooge. No.
Ch. Pres. (*severely*). You're not very *interested* in your clerk, are you ?
Scrooge. Why should I be ?
Ch. Pres. Well, that's his youngest. Tiny Tim.
Tiny Tim. Can I walk now, Papa ?
Cratchit (*patiently*). Not yet, Tiny Tim, there's too much snow. You'll fall and hurt yourself.
Tiny Tim (*indignantly*). I won't.
Cratchit. Oh, yes, you will, and then think what a bump you'd go. That would never do, would it ?
Tiny Tim (*solemnly*). No, that would never do. Then can I walk later ?
Cratchit. Perhaps.
Scrooge (*to the* Spirit). Why can't he let the boy walk now ? Making a mollycoddle of him. Cratchit's a fool, always was.
Ch. Pres. (*sternly*). Tiny Tim is a cripple ; he cannot walk as other children. (*He pauses.*) Is that answer enough ?
Scrooge (*subdued and ashamed*). Yes. I didn't know.
Ch. Pres. Mark this, Scrooge. If the shadows of the Future remain unaltered, if no hand is raised to help him, Tiny Tim will *die* !
Scrooge (*shaken*). No ! Kind Spirit, say he will be spared !
Ch. Pres. (*coolly*). Well, if he dies, what then ? It will help decrease the surplus population. Your own words, I think.

SCROOGE (*stepping on to the rostrum and crossing to* C.)
Cratchit !

(BOB CRATCHIT *begins to move off* L.)

CH. PRES.   He cannot hear you. See, they are going !

(BOB *exits* L. *with* TINY TIM.)

The surplus population ! Who are you to set yourself
above the judgment of God ? Will you decide what man
shall live and what shall die ? I say to you, in the sight of
Heaven, you are more worthless and less fit to live than
millions like that poor child. May God forgive you !

SCROOGE (*kneeling*).   Help me !
CH. PRES.   None can help you but yourself.

(*There is a loud burst of laughter from the darkness down* L.)

LIGHTING CUE : Bring up a spotlight down L. *and a*
firelight flood through the L.C. *arch.*)

(*A wing armchair is seen just below the* L.C. *arch. A small*
table stands R. *of it, with a bottle of sherry and two glasses.*
FRED, SCROOGE's nephew, enters through the arch with
AGNES, his young and pretty wife. He goes to sit in the
armchair, and AGNES sits at his feet, and rests her head
on his knees.)

FRED (*laughing*).   Yes, he did. He said that Christmas
was a humbug. He believed it, too.
AGNES.   More shame to him, then.
FRED.   He's a comical old fellow.
AGNES.   Comical !
FRED.   Oh, I grant you, not as pleasant as he might be,
and not so happy, either.
AGNES.   Well, he ought to be. He's very rich.
FRED (*teasing her*).   Is he now ?
AGNES.   You always say he is.
FRED.   What of it ? His money's no use to him. He
doesn't do any good with it. Doesn't even make *himself*
comfortable, let alone anyone else.
AGNES.   I've no patience with him.
FRED.   I have. I'm sorry for him.
AGNES (*quite annoyed for a moment*).   Sorry !

FRED. Yes. Couldn't be angry if I tried. Who suffers most from his bad temper ? Himself, of course !

AGNES (*sceptically*). How ?

FRED. Well, I asked him to dinner and he refused. So he loses a dinner. (*He grins at her.*) 'Course, it wasn't much of a dinner.

AGNES (*indignantly*). It was a very good dinner. I cooked every bit of it myself.

FRED. No wonder he refused.

AGNES. Don't be silly.

FRED. Sorry. No, all I meant was this. If Scrooge takes a dislike to me, or to anyone else for that matter, he loses a lot of pleasant moments and pleasant companions.

AGNES (*smiling*). You flatter yourself !

FRED. No, I don't. We're far better company than that mouldy old office of his. You should have seen what it looked like.

AGNES. I don't see why you had to go and see him at all.

FRED. My dear, I mean to give him the same chance every year, whether he likes it or not. Every Christmas Eve I'm going to that office to say " How are you, Uncle Scrooge. A Merry Christmas."

AGNES. And he'll say (*She imitates* SCROOGE). " Bah ! Humbug ! "

FRED. You never know. It might put him in a good enough humour to leave that poor clerk of his a few pounds in his will. Anyway, I think I shook him yesterday.

(*They laugh together.* FRED *kisses the top of her head.*)

Well, to the devil with old Scrooge !

AGNES. I'm sure he'd be very welcome.

SCROOGE (*offended*). Well, really !

FRED. Poor old Scrooge. He *is* a misery !

SCROOGE (*hurt*). I'm *not* !

FRED. You should have seen his face when I wished him a Merry Christmas. He looked down his nose, screwed up his eyes and said " What have you got to be so merry about. You're poor enough."

(*They laugh.*)

AGNES. Oh, well, *we* at least get a little fun out of him, even if *he* doesn't.

SCROOGE (*unhappily*). I want to go home !

FRED (*pouring two glasses of sherry*). Here, that's an idea ! He's made us laugh. It'd be ungrateful not to drink his health.

(*He rises, and gives a glass to* AGNES. *She also rises.*)

Uncle Scrooge !

AGNES. Well—(*She repeats the toast.*) Uncle Scrooge !

FRED. A Merry Christmas and a Happy New Year to the old—gentleman, wherever he is !

(*They raise their glasses and drink.*)

SCROOGE (*pleased by the toast*). Well, well ! (*He rubs his hands.*) Well, well, well !

LIGHTING CUE : *Take out the spotlight down* L. *and the firelight through* L.C. *arch.*

(AGNES *and* FRED *go off through the* L.C. *arch in the darkness.*)

(*The* SPIRIT *walks down the steps and turns to beckon* SCROOGE *after him.*)

CH. PRES. Come, we must go on !

SCROOGE (*following the* SPIRIT, *but peering still towards* L.C.). Oh, can't I stay and hear a bit more ?

EFFECTS CUE : *The church clock begins to strike twelve, and continues till the end of the* SPIRIT'S *next speech.*

(*The* SPIRIT *moves slowly down* C. *and* SCROOGE *follows.*)

The TRAVERSE CURTAIN *closes.*

CH. PRES. My time is nearly done. My life ends tonight. Each stroke of the clock brings death nearer. (*He begins to move backwards to the arch down* R.) Remember, Scrooge ! Remember those in want. Remember the sick, remember the ignorant, remember the poor! Remember Tiny Tim !

LIGHTING CUE : *The red spotlight on the* SPIRIT *fades out, and there is a Black-out.*

(*The* SPIRIT *disappears through the arch down* R.)

LIGHTING CUE : *Bring up the lights on the area round the bed.*

(SCROOGE *moves to the bed and sighs with relief.*) Well, he's gone ! (*He begins to smooth the sheets on the bed.*) No more ghosts !

LIGHTING CUE : *Bring up a white following spotlight* C. *on the* SPIRIT OF CHRISTMAS YET TO COME.

(*The* SPIRIT OF CHRISTMAS YET TO COME *enters* C. *of the Traverse Curtain. He wears a full-length dark grey robe with a hood and his face is covered with the mask of a skull. He crosses to the bed and stands just behind* SCROOGE. SCROOGE *continues to make the bed, finishes it to his satisfaction, climbs in, lies down and is about to go to sleep when he notices the* SPIRIT. *He leaps out of bed with a yell.*)

Here's another one ! (*He runs* C. *and falls on his knees.*) Speak to me !

(*The* SPIRIT *does not answer.*)

Are you the Spirit of Christmas Yet to Come ?

(*The* SPIRIT *does not answer.*)

You are to show me the future, the shadow of the things that await us in this life ?

(*The* SPIRIT *does not answer.*)

(*With anguish.*) Spirit, am I not right? (*He gets to his feet and gathers his courage.*) Ghost of the Future, I fear you more than anything I have yet seen, but I know you would do good to me. I will bear you company with a thankful heart. Will you not speak to me ?

(*The* SPIRIT *does not answer.*)

Then lead, and I will follow.

(*The* TRAVERSE CURTAIN *opens. The* SPIRIT *turns and moves upstage* R. *to the foot of the steps. He beckons* SCROOGE, *who follows and climbs the steps to the top. The rostrum is now bathed in a weird green-blue light. On* L. *of the rostrum are two gravestones silhouetted against the dark blue sky. One is a large rounded stone :* R. *of it is a small cross. A dark iron railing runs along the back of the rostrum, and beyond this can be seen part of the church and a distant view of the tall church spire.* BOB

D

CRATCHIT *stands* L. *of the small cross.* MRS. CRATCHIT *stands* R. *of it. They are dressed in mourning.* BOB *bends to place a small bunch of flowers against the cross.*)

MRS. CRATCHIT (*quietly*). "And he took a child and set him in the midst of them."
CRATCHIT. Come, my dear. We can do no more.
MRS. CRATCHIT (*weeping*). Why was he taken from us?
CRATCHIT. It was God's will. We shall come often. It will do us good to see how green a place it is.
MRS. CRATCHIT. I remember how you used to bring him here of a Sunday, perched on your shoulder.
CRATCHIT. He was that light to carry.
MRS. CRATCHIT (*moving behind the cross to* L.). We'll never forget him, none of us. Poor Tiny Tim, he was so patient.

(*They exit slowly off* L. *along the rostrum.*)

SCROOGE (*urgently*). "Tiny Tim!" Spirit, is it he that lies in the ground? Is it?
CH. TO COME (*in a hard, remote voice*). Yes.
SCROOGE (*appalled*). Why wasn't he spared? Is there no tenderness in Heaven?
CH. TO COME. Is there no tenderness in *you*? You could have saved him!
SCROOGE. It's too late!
CH. TO COME. No!
SCROOGE. What must I do? Tell me!
CH. TO COME. Only your heart can tell you. Listen!

(*The* SPIRIT *raises his arm and points down* L. SCROOGE *follows the direction of his arm.*)

LIGHTING CUE : *Bring up spotlight down* L.

(*A small table and three chairs are seen on the forestage down* L. *There are papers on the table. Two* BUSINESS MEN *in top hats and city clothes enter down* L. *talking.*)

1ST BUSINESS MAN (*going to the chair above the table*). Now let me see. Five thousand pounds for the shipment of the goods to Holland, and a further seven hundred pounds to cover the conveyance to Harwich. That seems to be in order, Mr. Plumstone. (*He sits.*)

2ND BUSINESS MAN (*sitting in the chair* R. *of the table*). Oh, perfectly in order, I assure you, Mr. Woolhead.

1ST BUSINESS MAN. And then there's the question of the transportation of the goods across Holland by canal. I understand that that will be the responsibility of your company . . .

(*The* THIRD BUSINESS MAN *enters through the arch down* L.)

3RD BUSINESS MAN. 'Afternoon, Woolhead, Plumstone.

1ST BUSINESS MAN ⎱
2ND BUSINESS MAN.⎰ (*together*).   Good afternoon.

1ST BUSINESS MAN.   Sit down, Mr. Blunderbone.

3RD BUSINESS MAN (*sitting* L. *of the table*).   Thank you. (*Very cheerfully*).   Well, gentleman, he's dead !

2ND BUSINESS MAN.   Ah, it doesn't surprise me, that it doesn't !

1ST BUSINESS MAN.   Was it soon over ?

3RD BUSINESS MAN.   Well, I don't know much about it either way. I only know that he's dead !

2ND BUSINESS MAN.   When did it happen ?

3RD BUSINESS MAN (*looking at his papers*).   Early this morning, I suppose.

1ST BUSINESS MAN.   What exactly was the matter with him ? I thought he was never going to die.

3RD BUSINESS MAN (*yawning*).   God knows !

2ND BUSINESS MAN.   What's he done with his money ?

3RD BUSINESS MAN.   I haven't heard. Left it to his company, I suppose.

1ST BUSINESS MAN.   Well, one thing's certain. He hasn't left it to *us* !

(*They roar with laughter at the idea.*)

2ND BUSINESS MAN.   It's likely to be a cheap funeral. He was a mean, cantankerous old miser, if ever there was one.

(*They all agree.*)

1ST BUSINESS MAN.   I don't suppose many will go to it. Can't think of anyone who'd want to !

(*They all laugh again.*)

3RD BUSINESS MAN.   Well, *someone* ought to go. We might get up a party and volunteer.

2ND BUSINESS MAN (*dubious*).   Well, I don't mind going if lunch is provided. But I must be fed if I go.

(*They laugh.*)

3RD BUSINESS MAN. Well, well, we'll go if we can't think of anything more interesting to do. But I don't like funerals, especially in this weather.

1ST BUSINESS MAN (*putting his feet on the table*).   Catch your death of cold.

2ND BUSINESS MAN (*putting his feet on the table*).   Depressing, too. Spoil my Christmas.

3RD BUSINESS MAN (*putting his feet on the table*).   'Tisn't as if he'd ever done anything for us, is it ?

1ST BUSINESS MAN.   Poor old chap ! (*He yawns.*)

2ND BUSINESS MAN.   Very sad ! (*He yawns.*)

3RD BUSINESS MAN.   Such a pity ! (*He yawns.*)

1ST BUSINESS MAN.   We ought to go—really . . . (*He drops off to sleep and snores loudly.*)

2ND BUSINESS MAN.   Out of common decency. (*He drops off to sleep and snores loudly.*)

3RD BUSINESS MAN.   After all, he *is* dead ! (*He drops off to sleep and snores loudly.*)

(*They all snore together.*)

LIGHTING CUE : *Take out spotlight down* L.

SCROOGE (*turning to the* SPIRIT).   Well, they don't seem very sorry for the old gentleman, whoever he is.

CH. TO COME.   They're not.

SCROOGE.   Who is it that's died ?

CH. TO COME (*in a strange voice*).   You'll know—some day.

SCROOGE (*more interested*).   It might be someone I know.

CH. TO COME (*in the same voice*).   It is !

SCROOGE (*sensing that the* SPIRIT *means something of importance to him*).   Tell me his name !

(*The* SPIRIT *does not answer.*)

Tell me his name ! (*He begins to plead.*) Spirit, I feel our parting is at hand. The case of that unhappy soul might be my own. Tell me ! Who is the man that is dead !

CH.·TO COME (*slowly*).   If you would know, go up into the churchyard. A cold stone covers his grave. On the stone is the name of the man.

(SCROOGE *turns and looks towards the large gravestone.*)

SCROOGE (*pointing*).   Is that the stone ?

CH. TO COME.   Yes !

(SCROOGE *moves along the rostrum towards the tombstone.*)

LIGHTING CUE : Switch on the tombstone effect.

(*The name* SCROOGE *is suddenly illuminated on the stone.* SCROOGE *recoils with horror.*)

SCROOGE (*screaming*). No ! (*He turns towards the* SPIRIT (*Breathlessly*). Why do you show me this ?   Have I no hope? Spirit, I am not the man I was. Have you changed my life, opened the gates to charity and kindness, only to cast me into the bitterness of death. Let me have time ! Let me repay the wrongs I have done ! Let me atone !

(*The* SPIRIT *makes no sign.*)

(SCROOGE *continues desperately.*)   I will honour Christmas in my heart ; I will do more. I will strive to keep it all the year. I will live in the Past, the Present and the Future ! (*He kneels.*) I have seen ! I have heard ! I have learnt what the spirits would teach me ! Tell me I may tear away the writing on the stone ! (*He turns to the stone and raises his fingers as though he would scrape away the writing. He weeps.*) No ! No ! No !

(*The* SPIRIT *disappears through the arch* R.C. SCROOGE *lies sobbing at the foot of the stone*).

LIGHTING CUE : Dawn begins to break over the cemetery. The sky glows red and lightens until a strong beam of sunlight falls on SCROOGE *below the tombstone.*

EFFECTS CUE : The sound of voices singing " Come, all ye Faithful ! " is heard from the church and grows slowly louder.

LIGHTING CUE : As the general light increases, slowly fade out the tombstone effect.

(SCROOGE *stirs, raises his head, pulls himself to his knees and extends his arms longingly towards the great light that is flooding him.*)

EFFECTS CUE : *The carol grows to its climax as—*

The CURTAIN *falls.*

ACT III

SCENE I

SCENE.—*The street outside the office of* SCROOGE AND MARLEY. *Morning.*

A frontcloth painted to represent a row of London houses blanketed with snow hangs just behind the false proscenium. (*Alternatively, the Traverse Curtain may be used.*) *A snow-laden lamp-post stands down* R.

When the CURTAIN *rises, a ragged* LAD *of about fifteen is leaning against the lamp-post, chewing a straw.* SCROOGE *runs on through the arch down* L. *He is in tremendously good spirits, and is a new and much improved man. He stops* L. *of* C.

SCROOGE (*rubbing his hands*). Wonderful day ! Glorious ! I never felt so young in my life ! (*He sees the* LAD.) Hey ! Boy !

LAD (*turning his head; stolidly*). Uh ?

SCROOGE. Come here!

LAD (*slowly lounging over to* SCROOGE). Uh ?

SCROOGE. Now tell me ! What's today ?

LAD (*not very bright*). Eh ?

SCROOGE. What's *today*, my fine fellow ?

LAD (*taking the straw from his mouth*). Oh, you mean, " What's today ? "

SCROOGE. Yes.

LAD (*stolidly*). It's Christmas Day.

SCROOGE (*delighted*). Christmas Day ! I haven't missed it !

LAD (*surprised*). Eh ?

SCROOGE (*jumping about with glee*). The Spirits have done it all in one night. They can do anything they like.

LAD. Spirits ?

SCROOGE (*approaching him and patting him on the back*). Of course they can ! (*He turns away down* L. *and rubs his hands.*)

LAD (*putting back his straw*). Strikes me you've 'ad a drop of spirits yerself, aven't you ?

SCROOGE (*turning and looking at him as if for the first time.*) Hullo, my fine fellow !

LAD. 'Aven't we just met ?

SCROOGE (*cackling merrily*). Droll. Oh, very droll.

LAD (*unmoved*). I'm busting me sides.

SCROOGE. Now, listen. Do you know the poulterer's in the next street but one, at the corner ?

LAD. I should hope I do.

SCROOGE. An intelligent boy ! A sensible boy ! Now, do you know whether they've sold the prize turkey that was hanging outside ?

LAD. You mean the . . .

SCROOGE. Oh, not the little turkey. The big one. (*He rubs his hands*). The *expensive* one !

LAD. It's still there orlright !

SCROOGE. It is ? Go and buy it !

LAD. Right-o ! (*He starts to move to the* R., *stops, and turns angrily*). 'Ere, what's the idea ? Are you trying ter . . .

SCROOGE (*moving to him at* R.C.). No, no, I mean it. Go and buy it. And tell them to send it to Bob Cratchit, at 42 Primrose Lane. And then come back and tell me you've done it. If you're back within five minutes, I'll give you a shilling.

LAD. What abaht paying for the turkey ?

SCROOGE (*airily*). Tell them Mr. Scrooge sent you.

LAD. Mr. Scrooge ! Blimey, they'll never believe that !

(*He runs off down* R.)

SCROOGE (*calling after him*). The big one, mind, not the little one ! (*He rubs his hands.*) Oh, Bob Cratchit *will* be pleased. It's twice the size of Tiny Tim !

(*The* TWO PORTLY GENTLEMEN *from Act One enter through the arch down* L. *and cross slowly to* C.)

(SCROOGE *turns, sees them, moves to* C. *and holds out his hand to the* FIRST PORTLY GENTLEMAN.) My dear sir !

(*The* FIRST PORTLY GENTLEMAN *ignores the outstretched hand and passes him to down* R.)

(SCROOGE *offers his hand to the* SECOND PORTLY GENTLE-MAN.)　My dear sir !

(*The* SECOND PORTLY GENTLEMAN *ignores him and passes him to down* R.)

(*He turns and calls after them.*)　Gentlemen, I beg you to listen !

(*The* TWO PORTLY GENTLEMEN *stop and turn to him.*)

1ST PORT. GENT. (*stiffly*).　Well ?
2ND PORT. GENT. (*stiffly*).　Well ?
SCROOGE (*embarrassed*).　Well . . .
1ST PORT. GENT.　Mr. Scrooge, I believe ?
2ND PORT. GENT.　Of Scrooge and Marley's !
SCROOGE (*humbly*).　Yes.　How do you do ?　I hope you succeeded in your mission yesterday.　It was so kind of you.　(*He makes a tremendous effort.*)　A—a Merry Christmas to you both !

(*The* PORTLY GENTLEMEN *are amazed.*)

1ST PORT. GENT. (*after a pause*).　It *is* Mr. Scrooge, isn't it ?
2ND PORT. GENT.　Of Scrooge and Marley's ?
SCROOGE.　That is my name, and I fear it may not be very pleasant to you.
1ST PORT. GENT.　Well . . .
2ND PORT. GENT.　Well . . .
SCROOGE.　My dear sir, allow me to ask your pardon, and yours, sir.
2ND PORT. GENT.　Yes, yes, of course.
SCROOGE (*moving close to the* FIRST PORTLY GENTLEMAN). And one thing more.　Your collections for charity.　If I may be allowed to donate . . . (*He whispers in the ear of the* FIRST PORTLY GENTLEMAN, *who is astounded.*)
1ST PORT. GENT.　Lord bless me ! (*To the* SECOND PORT. GENT.)　He wishes to be allowed to donate . . . (*He whispers in the ear of the* SECOND PORTLY GENTLEMAN, *who is in turn astounded.*)
2ND PORT. GENT.　My dear Mr. Scrooge !　Are you serious ?
SCROOGE.　If you please.

1ST PORT. GENT. It seems such a large sum.

2ND PORT. GENT. It *is* such a large sum !

SCROOGE. Not a farthing less ! You see, a great many back payments are included.

1ST PORT. GENT (*shaking* SCROOGE's *hand*). My dear sir, I don't know what to say to such generosity !

SCROOGE. Don't say anything, please. Oh, and one thing more ! I wish to remain anonymous.

1ST PORT. GENT. Of course, if you wish it . . .

SCROOGE. I do.

2ND PORT. GENT. Very well. And thank you once more, sir.

SCROOGE. Not at all, sir. (*To the* FIRST PORTLY GENTLEMAN.) Pray come and see me one day.

1ST PORT. GENT. With the greatest of pleasure.

SCROOGE (*to the* SECOND PORTLY GENTLEMAN). And will *you* come and see me, too ?

2ND PORT. GENT. (*heartily*). I will, sir.

SCROOGE. Thank you, thank you. I'm much obliged to you.

1ST PORT. GENT. On the contrary, *we* are much obliged to *you*.

2ND PORT. GENT. (*raising his hat*). And a Merry Christmas to you, sir !

1ST PORT. GENT. (*raising his hat*). And a Happy New Year !

SCROOGE (*raising his hat*). Thank you, gentlemen, and the same to you both !

(*They all replace their hats.*)

And now, gentlemen, I must leave you.

1ST PORT. GENT. Good day, Mr. Scrooge.

SCROOGE (*going* L.). Good day ! (*He stops and turns.*) And don't forget ! I wish to remain anonymous !

(*He goes out down* L. *The* PORTLY GENTLEMEN *move to* C., *and look after him.*)

1ST PORT. GENT. Well, who would have thought it !

2ND PORT. GENT. Most amazing ! Mr. Scrooge, of all people !

1ST PORT. GENT. (*taking out his list*). Now then, shall we see how much we've collected ?

2ND PORT. GENT. (*taking out his list ; eagerly*).   Yes.

(*They run their fingers up and down the columns of figures on their papers together. They mutter the figures in unison as they add. Finally the* FIRST GENTLEMAN *turns to the* SECOND.)

1ST PORT. GENT.   What do you make it ?
2ND PORT. GENT. (*showing his paper*).   Well, I make it . . .
1ST PORT. GENT. (*showing his paper; delighted*).   So do I !
2ND PORT. GENT.   And with Mr. Scrooge's contribution it will be . . . (*He points to the list again.*)
1ST PORT. GENT.   So it will !
2ND PORT. GENT.   We mustn't forget to have the list published as soon as possible.
1ST PORT. GENT.   Yes. Except for Mr. Scrooge. He wishes to remain anonymous.
2ND PORT. GENT.   But that hardly seems fair. Mr. Scrooge has given *most*.
1ST PORT. GENT (*agreeing*).   Yes, Mr. Scrooge has given most.

(*The orchestra plays a chord, and they sing the song " Mr. Scrooge has given most." They make all gestures and movements in unison. During the chorus after each verse they dance round each other with arms linked, and persuade the audience to join in the singing of the chorus.*)

Air : " *Come Landlord, fill the flowing bowl.*"
1ST and 2ND PORT. GENT.
    "We've been collecting, so to speak
    We've raised a lot of money
    We're going to give the poor a week
    Of flowing milk and honey "
CHORUS
    " But Mr. Scrooge has given most
    Mr. Scrooge has given most
    Mr. Scrooge has given most
    He's given . . . . .SHH ！

(*They mouth the last words of the chorus silently. The last beat is a loud " Ssh ! " to the audience.*)

1ST PORT. GENT.   " Now Mr. Snodgrass gave us four
                 And Mr. Tupkins plenty.

2ND PORT. GENT.	And Mr. Pickwick gave us more Which brought it up to twenty "
CHORUS	" But Mr. Scrooge, etc . . . "
2ND PORT. GENT.	" We called on David Copperfield And he gave us a shilling.
1ST PORT. GENT.	We asked old Barkis if he'd yield And he said he was willing."
CHORUS	"But Mr. Scrooge, etc . . . "
1ST PORT GENT.	" Uriah Heep turned down the lamp And said ' I'm very 'umble ! '
2ND PORT. GENT.	Mrs. Gamp gave us a stamp And so did Mr. Bumble."
CHORUS	"But Mr. Scrooge, etc . . . "
2ND PORT. GENT.	" With Mr. Squeers we had a job And Bill Sykes gave us curses.
1ST PORT. GENT.	The Artful Dodger gave a bob And then he stole our purses."
CHORUS	"But Mr. Scrooge, etc . . . "
1ST PORT. GENT.	" We called on Martin Chuzzlewit And asked for a donation
2ND PORT. GENT.	And even Fagin gave a bit Which caused a great sensation."

(*They sing the last chorus in harmony, arm in arm, with their hats tucked under their other arms.*)

> " But Mr. Scrooge has given most
> Mr. Scrooge has given most
> Mr. Scrooge has given most
> He's given . . . .

(*They are about to tell the audience how much* MR. SCROOGE *has given.* SCROOGE *himself runs on down* L.)

SCROOGE (*warning*). Eh !

(*The* PORTLY GENTLEMEN *turn their heads quickly and see* SCROOGE. *Turning back, they ' cake walk ' off* R. *to the last line of the song.*)

1ST and 2ND PORT. GENT. (*dancing off*). " He's given la la *la* SHH ! "

(SCROOGE *moves* C. *and watches them go.* FRED, SCROOGE'S *nephew, enters through the arch down* L. *He stops and turns to light a cigar.* SCROOGE *creeps towards him and slaps him on the back.*)

SCROOGE.   A Merry Christmas, Nephew !

(FRED *splutters over the ruins of his cigar.*)

FRED (*recovering and turning to* SCROOGE). Good Heavens ! It's . . .

SCROOGE.   Your Uncle Scrooge !

FRED (*amazed*).   So it is ! (*He pauses.*) *What* did you say just now ?

SCROOGE.   I said " Merry Christmas."

FRED.   That's what I thought you said. (*He looks intently at* SCROOGE.) Are you feeling quite well, Uncle ?

SCROOGE.   Never felt better in my life. How's your charming wife ? Pray give her my kindest regards.

FRED (*dazed*).   I must be dreaming.

SCROOGE.   No, it's *I* who have been dreaming. (*He takes a cigar from his pocket.*) Pray accept a cigar ! (*He hands it to* FRED.)

FRED (*taking it automatically*).   It must have been a wonderful dream to put you in this humour.

SCROOGE.   It was, it was. (*He takes out another cigar.*) Have *another* cigar !

FRED (*taking it*).   Thank you.

SCROOGE.   Now, listen. You can do something for *me*.

FRED (*cautiously*).   Oh ? What ?

SCROOGE.   You can invite me to dinner—tonight !

FRED (*laughing*).   Come to dinner tonight.

SCROOGE.   I accept !

(*The* LAD *runs on through the arch down* R. *and stops* R.C.)

LAD.   Here I am, Mr. Scrooge !

SCROOGE (*crossing to him*).   Ah, excellent. Did you buy the turkey ?

LAD.   Yus.

SCROOGE.   The big one ?

LAD.   Yus !

SCROOGE.   Are they sending it to the address I gave you ?

LAD.   Yus !

SCROOGE.   Wonderful boy !

LAD.   Yus ! 'Ere, I was back in five minutes. What abaht my shilling ?

SCROOGE (*pretending not to understand*).   Shilling ?

LAD.   Yus, yer promised me a shilling.

SCROOGE. Nonsense, boy, I'm not going to give you a shilling.

LAD (*blankly*). No?

SCROOGE. No, I'm going to give you half a crown. (*He takes a half crown from his pocket and throws it to the* LAD.) Here. Off you go!

LAD (*looking at the coin with amazement*). Blimey, must be the end of the world!

(*He goes out down* R.)

FRED (*approaching* SCROOGE). Uncle, are you *sure* you're feeling all right?

SCROOGE. Certainly, my boy. Capital! Oh, here, I forgot. (*He takes out some more money and gives it to* FRED.) Get that delightful wife of yours something for Christmas.

FRED (*stunned*). "Delightful wife!" But you've never even met her.

SCROOGE. Never mind, she must be delightful. You married her, didn't you?

FRED. Yes, I married her.

SCROOGE (*crossing to* L. *of* FRED). Good-bye, my boy, till tonight.

FRED. Here, Uncle, why not come back with me now and meet her?

SCROOGE. No time. I'm off to Bob Cratchit's.

FRED. Cratchit. Uncle, you're not going to make him work today!

SCROOGE. Work! What a preposterous idea! Nobody works today. It's Christmas Day!

(*He walks off jauntily down* L. FRED *stares after him in amazement.*)

LIGHTING CUE: *Black-out.*

EFFECTS CUE: *The music of " Sir Roger de Coverley " swells up.*

(*The* TRAVERSE CURTAIN *opens in darkness.*)

SCENE.—*The parlour in* BOB CRATCHIT'S *house. The time is immediately following the previous scene.*

The room is decorated with red and yellow wallpaper patterned with red and blue flowers, and some cheap but cheerful pictures of flowers and country scenes hang on the wall. The front door is down L. *Above this the side-wall is pierced by a window with chintz curtains and a chintz-covered window seat on which lie several cushions. There is a sideboard up* C. *It carries dishes of china and pewter, and a small, scantily-dressed Christmas tree. Up* R. *a door leads to the kitchen. Down* R. *there is a large cowled fireplace, in front of which lies a rag rug. A Windsor chair with arms stands at the top end of the fireplace : below it is a small oak stool. A large table stands* C. *in the room, ready for the Christmas meal of the* CRATCHIT *family of seven. Three wheelback chairs are above it, a chair stands at either end, and there is an oak bench below it. The table is laid for seven with knives, forks and spoons. Two mugs stand stand* C. *of the table, and the carving-knife and fork are at the* L. *end. The room gives an impression of comfort and cosiness, even though it has seen better days.*

(*See the Ground Plan at the end of the play.*)

When the lights fade in PETER CRATCHIT, *the second eldest child, is busy putting a log on the fire. The two young* CRATCHIT *girls,* SARAH *and* BELINDA, *are up* L. *battling with cushions taken from the window seat, and making a considerable amount of noise.*

BELINDA (*hitting out with her cushion and driving* SARAH *down* L.). I'm winning ! I'm winning !

SARAH (*retreating below* C. *of the table*). You're not ! You cheated ! You hit me when I wasn't ready.

BELINDA (*following her*). I'm going to knock your head right off !

PETER (*expostulating*). Do stop it. Mama will come in !

(SARAH *bumps into him and knocks him off his balance as she passes round the* R. *end of the table.*)

Don't *do* that !

(*He gets up, but* BELINDA *sends him flying again as she passes round the* R. *end of the table.* SARAH *retreats above the table to the window-seat.*)

I said, don't do that!

(BELINDA *reaches the* L. *end of the table again. She dives underneath it and crawls along to the* R. SARAH *also dives under the table.*)

BELINDA. I'm a train in a tunnel! You can't catch me!
SARAH. Yes, I can! I'm another train!

(BELINDA *and* SARAH *crawl out from under* R. *end of the table and collide once more with* PETER. *A pitched battle follows between the three of them, and all shout.* MRS. CRATCHIT *hurries in through the kitchen door up* R. *She is a pleasant-looking woman of fifty and a capable and sensible mother.*)

MRS. CRATCHIT. Now, stop it, children! *Stop it!*

(*The children stop fighting.* BELINDA *and* SARAH *run down* L. *and stand looking innocent with their cushions held behind them.* PETER *moves* C. *of the fireplace.* MRS. CRATCHIT *crosses to the sideboard and brings some more things from it to the table.*)

BELINDA (*airily*). It was Peter's fault. He began it.
PETER (*indignant*). I didn't.
SARAH. You did! You did!
BELINDA (*imitating a schoolmistress*). A most unruly child! Something will have to be done about the boy!
PETER. Oh, shut up! (*He goes to sit on the fireside stool.*)
MRS. CRATCHIT (*placidly setting the last few things on the table*). Now, that's enough from all of you. (*She looks at* BELINDA.) Belinda!
BELINDA. Yes, Mama?
MRS. CRATCHIT. What have you got behind your back?
BELINDA (*innocently*). Oh, just an old cushion.
MRS. CRATCHIT. I see! Sarah!
SARAH. Yes, Mama?

MRS. CRATCHIT. What have *you* got?

SARAH. Oh, just another old cushion.

MRS. CRACHIT. I thought so. Well put them back where they belong, and try and be good for a change.

(*The girls take the cushions back to the window-seat. BELINDA gives SARAH a surreptitious bang en route.*)

(*Busy at the table.*) I can't think what's happened to your father and Tiny Tim. I do hope they're not going to be late.

BELINDA (*coming to* L. *of her mother behind the table*). Mama, can I go and look at the goose?

MRS. CRATCHIT. Not yet, Bella. It isn't quite done.

SARAH. *When* is it done? (*She moves to* L. *of* BELINDA.)

MRS. CRATCHIT. Bless the child! I don't know. When it *looks* done.

SARAH. Do you know it's done when you look at it?

MRS. CRATCHIT. Yes.

BELINDA. Then why can't *I* look at it and see if it's done?

MRS. CRATCHIT (*moving to below the* R. *end of the table, distracted*). You can in a minute. Peter, did you get the logs for the fire?

PETER. Yes, Mama.

MRS. CRATCHIT. That's a good boy. Belinda, look out of the window and see if Martha's coming. She's never been as late as this before on Christmas Day.

BELINDA (*going to the window and looking out*). Here's Martha *now*!

(SARAH *and* BELINDA *rush to the door down* L. *and scramble to open it. MARTHA, the eldest of the* CRATCHIT *children, enters. She is pretty and almost grown up, but she looks overworked and tired.*)

MARTHA (*to the girls*). Hallo, Bella, Sarah! (*She crosses to her mother below the table.*) Hallo, Mama. (*She kisses her mother.*)

MRS. CRATCHIT. Bless my heart alive, how late you are! We thought you weren't coming.

(SARAH *and* BELINDA *move to above the table.*)

MARTHA. Of course I was.

E

MRS. CRATCHIT.   Take off your cloak and bonnet, dear.

(MARTHA *takes off her cloak and bonnet and moves up* L. *to the window-seat to put them down.*)

BELINDA.   We've got an enormous goose.

SARAH.   It's the biggest goose in the world.

PETER (*superior*).   Don't be silly. Geese are all the same size. Like ducks.

BELINDA.   They're not !

SARAH.   Anyway, I saw a small duck once.

(SARAH *and* BELINDA *move to the window.*)

MARTHA (*coming to below* L. *end of the table*).   We'd a deal of work to finish up last night. We had to clear away this morning.

MRS. CRATCHIT.   It's a shame the way they work you in that place.

MARTHA.   Might be worse.

MRS. CRATCHIT.   And it might be better. Come and sit by the fire, dear, and get warm. Make room, Peter.

(MARTHA *begins crossing to the fireplace.* PETER *moves his feet from the hearth.*)

BELINDA (*turning from the window*).   Here's father coming !

SARAH (*looking out*).   He's crossing the road.

BELINDA (*coming to above the table*).   Hide, Martha, and surprise him !

(*They all agree noisily.*)

MARTHA (*laughing*).   All right. Where shall I hide ?

SARAH.   Below the door.

BELINDA.   Quick ! He'll see you !

SARAH.   Hurry up !

(MARTHA *rushes across the stage to below the front door, and hides.* SARAH *joins* BELINDA *above the table, and* MRS. CRATCHIT *moves to* R. *of the table. They stand waiting. After a few moments the door opens.* BOB CRATCHIT *enters, carrying* TINY TIM *on his shoulder. He comes* C. *below the table.*)

BOB.   Here we are !

TINY TIM.   Here we are !

MRS. CRATCHIT. Bob Cratchit, I thought you'd gone to China, you've been that long.

BOB (*mildly*). I'm sorry, my dear.

TINY TIM. I want to get down.

BOB. And so you shall, you giant ! Here, you can sit in my chair and carve the goose ! (*He carries* TINY TIM *to the chair at the* L. *end of the table and sits him down.*)

(BELINDA *takes* TINY TIM'S *crutch and puts it on the sideboard up* C.)

TINY TIM (*examining the table*). Where's the goose ?

SARAH. It's waiting to be *looked* at.

CRATCHIT (*looking round*). Hello, where's Martha ?

(*There is a pause.*)

MRS. CRATCHIT (*slowly*). Martha ? Oh, she's not coming.

CRATCHIT (*after a slight pause*). Not coming ? Not coming on Christmas Day ?

(SARAH *and* BELINDA *begin to giggle.* MARTHA *approaches* BOB, *who turns and sees her.*)

Martha ! (*He hugs her.*) Not coming indeed !

BELINDA. Mama, is it time to look at the goose ?

MRS. CRATCHIT. All right, run along, Only don't touch it.

BELINDA (*to* SARAH). I'll race you.

(*She rushes off through the door up* R.)

SARAH (*following her*). You started before me.

(*She rushes off up* R.)

MRS. CRATCHIT. Peter, you go and keep an eye on them. They'll have it on the floor in two minutes.

PETER (*rising and going up* R.). Yes, Mama. (*He goes through the door.*) Mama says you're not to *touch* it . . .

(*He Exits up* R.)

CRATCHIT (*to* MRS. CRATCHIT, *unwinding his scarf*). I met Mr. Scrooge's nephew on the High Road. He asked after you.

(MARTHA *goes to* TINY TIM *and kisses him.*)

MRS. CRATCHIT (*pleased*). Did he ?

CRATCHIT. Yes. " How's your good wife ? " he said to me. Now, I wonder how he knew that.

MRS. CRATCHIT. What ?

CRATCHIT (*going to her below the table*). That you're a good wife.

TINY TIM (*solemnly*). Everyone knows that.

CRATCHIT (*turning to him*). Well said, you rascal, I should hope they do. (*He turns back to* MRS. CRATCHIT.) He asked how Peter was getting along and said if he could be of service, he would. I shouldn't be surprised if he didn't mean to help him to a better situation. (*He takes his wife's arm and leads her to the fire.*)

TINY TIM (*loudly*). I've got a box of bricks for Christmas. Mama, can I show them to Martha ?

MRS. CRATCHIT. Of course you can. Martha, they're on the dresser there.

(MARTHA *goes up* C. *to fetch the bricks and brings them to the* L. *end of the table. She sits in the chair above the table next to* TINY TIM.)

TINY TIM (*chattily*). There are red ones and green ones and yellow ones.

MARTHA (*showing him one*). And blue ones. (*She helps him to build a house.*)

MRS. CRATCHIT (*sitting on the stool below the fire*). How did Tiny Tim behave ?

CRATCHIT (*sitting in the armchair*). As good as gold.

MRS. CRATCHIT. Asking questions, I'll be bound.

CRATCHIT. No, he was quiet today. He comes out with the strangest things sometimes.

MRS. CRATCHIT. Yes. It's with sitting alone so much ; makes him thoughtful.

CRATCHIT (*quietly*). Today, just as we were coming through the churchyard, he said he hoped people would see him in church. Just suddenly, like that.

MRS. CRATCHIT. Why ?

CRATCHIT. Because it was Christmas Day. He thought, as he was a cripple, it might help them to remember that it was the birthday of One who made the blind see, and the lame walk.

MRS. CRATCHIT (*quietly*).   Yes.

CRATCHIT (*rising and pulling* MRS. CRATCHIT *to him*). Now, now, don't worry your heart out ! Why, he gets stronger every day.

(BELINDA *rushes in up* R. *from the kitchen, followed by* SARAH.)

BELINDA.   Mama ! The pudding !

MRS. CRATCHIT (*startled*).   What's happened to it ?

SARAH.   It's making funny noises.

MRS. CRATCHIT (*alarmed*).   What sort of noises ?

BELINDA.   Gurgles.

SARAH.   And plops !

BELINDA.   It's going to explode.

SARAH.   Peter says we must pour cold water on it.

MRS. CRATCHIT (*rushing up* R. *to the kitchen door*).   Good Heavens, he'll ruin it. (*She goes out, calling.*) Peter, put down that jug !

TINY TIM (*unmoved by the excitement*).   Look at my house !

(*The girls move* C. *above the table to look.*)

Martha made it.

MARTHA.   We both made it.

BELINDA (*critically*).   It hasn't got a roof.

TINY TIM.   I don't want a roof.

SARAH.   Silly ! It must have a roof or the rain'll come in.

TINY TIM (*finally*).   It isn't raining.

(PETER *enters and goes down* R. *below the fire.*)

PETER.   Mama says the dinner'll be ten minutes.

CRATCHIT (*lifting a large jug of punch from the fireplace*). Never mind, the punch is ready. Get your cups, all of you. We'll warm ourselves while we wait. (*He begins to fill the three mugs that stand on the mantelpiece.*)

(BELINDA *and* SARAH *tussle over the mugs on the table.* MARTHA *rises and goes to the sideboard* C.)

BELINDA (*struggling*).   That's *my* mug !

SARAH.   It isn't ! It's mine !

(SARAH *secures the mug and moves round the table to sit on the bench below it.* BELINDA *takes the other mug from the centre of the table and sits above the* R. *end of the table.* MARTHA *picks up a pewter mug from the sideboard.*)

E*

MARTHA. I'll have this one.

TINY TIM. What do I have ?

MARTHA (*picking up an eggcup from the sideboard*). Here you are. (*She brings it to his place.*) This is yours.

TINY TIM (*objecting*). It's an eggcup. I want a big one.

CRATCHIT. You can have two lots.

(MRS. CRATCHIT *comes in through the kitchen door up* R. BOB *hands her a mug of punch. She takes it and goes to sit at the* R. *end of the table.* BOB *gives another full mug to* PETER.)

Now then, hold out your cups. (*He carries his own full mug in one hand and the jug of punch in the other. He goes to* BELINDA's *place to fill her mug.*)

(BELINDA *starts to drink at once.*)

No, wait, Belinda ! We'll have a toast in a minute. (*He moves along the table and fills* SARAH's *mug,* MARTHA's *mug and* TINY TIM's *eggcup.*) And one for Tiny Tim !

TINY TIM. Full up !

CRATCHIT. Right over the top ! (*He moves to* L.C.) Now, let's have a toast. (*He raises his mug and offers the toast.*) A Merry Christmas to us all ? God bless us !

TINY TIM (*piping*). God bless us, every one !

(*They all drink.* BOB *crosses below the table to the fireplace.*)

CRATCHIT. And now we'll have a game.

(*Everyone shouts agreement.*)

What shall it be ?

BELINDA. Hunt the slipper !

SARAH. No, you're too rough.

PETER. Hunt the slipper !

MARTHA (*glancing at* TINY TIM). No, let's have something we can all play.

MRS. CRATCHIT (*vaguely*). What about that game where one of you—er—goes into the other room—no, all the others go into the next room, well, it doesn't matter really—and the ones who go out have to think of—no, it's the other one who thinks—I think—well, you know what I mean. Something to do with history.

(*General laughter and shouts of* " No ! ", " Just like Mama ! ")

CRATCHIT. I've got it. Let's play " Yes and No."

(*Everyone agrees.* MRS. CRATCHIT *looks puzzled.*)

MRS. CRATCHIT. " Yes and No ? " I don't quite remember how . . .

MARTHA. Oh, you know, Mama. Someone thinks of a person, or an object, or anything at all, and the others have to guess what it is.

BELINDA. And you can only answer " Yes " or " No " to the questions.

SARAH. But you can ask any questions.

MARTHA. Do you see, Mama ?

MRS. CRATCHIT (*fogged*). Well . . .

MARTHA. You'll remember all right as we go along. Now, who's going to think of something ?

TINY TIM. *I* am !

MARTHA. No, you go second.

SARAH. Let papa go first.

BELINDA. He always thinks of good ones.

CRATCHIT. Wait a minute, now. (*He thinks.*) All right, I've thought of something. One, two, three, GO !

(*They all start to fire questions at breakneck speed.*)

BELINDA. Is it vegetable ?

CRATCHIT. No.

SARAH. Mineral ?

CRATCHIT. No.

MARTHA. Animal ?

CRATCHIT. Yes !

PETER. It's an animal. Is it alive ?

CRATCHIT. Yes.

MRS. CRATCHIT. Is it a wild animal ?

CRATCHIT. No.

MRS. CRATCHIT (*disappointed*). Not a wild animal. I thought it might be a whale.

TINY TIM (*suddenly*). It's a cat !

CRATCHIT. No.

TINY TIM (*logically*). A cat's an animal.

SARAH. Silly.

MARTHA. Is it a nice animal ?

CRATCHIT. No.

MRS. CRATCHIT (*off on a new track*). Does it make grunting noises ?

CRATCHIT (*not quite certain*). Yes.

MARTHA. Grunting noises. Is it a pig ?

CRATCHIT. No.

BELINDA. Does it live in England.?

CRATCHIT. Yes.

PETER. Does it live in a cage ?

CRATCHIT. No.

TINY TIM (*positive*). It's a cat !

EVERYONE. No.

SARAH. A cat doesn't grunt.

MRS. CRATCHIT. I remember a cat that *did* make sort of grunting noises.

BELINDA (*desperate*). Mama ! It isn't a cat.

PETER (*restoring order*). It's an animal that isn't nice, makes grunting noises, lives in London but not in a cage.

BELINDA. Do you eat it ?

CRATCHIT (*laughing*). No.

TINY TIM. It's a cow.

CRATCHIT. No.

MARTHA. How many legs ? Has it got four legs ?

CRATCHIT. No.

MRS. CRATCHIT (*suddenly brilliant*). Has it got three legs ? (*She reflects.*) No, it couldn't have, could it ? Poor thing !

SARAH. Two legs ?

CRATCHIT. Yes.

MARTHA. Two legs, grunts, lives in London, and isn't nice.

BELINDA. A monkey ?

SARAH. A duck ?

MRS. CRATCHIT. A squirrel ?

PETER. A kangeroo ?

MARTHA (*suddenly*). I know what it is !

EVERYONE. WHAT ?

MARTHA. It's Mr. Scrooge !

CRATCHIT. Yes !

(*They all laugh.*)

MARTHA. Poor Mr. Scrooge, he doesn't really grunt !

SARAH. Anyway, he's got *four* legs. He's a bear.

TINY TIM (*busy with his bricks*). Was it a cat ?

MARTHA. No.

TINY TIM (*pleased*).　I said it was.

CRATCHIT.　Well, we've had some fun out of the old gentleman. Now let's give him a toast. (*He raises his glass.*) To Mr. Scrooge, the founder of the feast !

MRS. CRATCHIT (*warmly*).　Founder of the feast, indeed ? I wish I had him here. I'd give him a piece of my mind to feast on. And I hope he'd have a good appetite for it.

CRATCHIT (*mildly*).　My dear, it's Christmas.

MRS. CRATCHIT.　I should think it must be when we drink the health of such an odious, stingy, unfeeling man as Mr. Scrooge.

CRATCHIT.　Now, now.

MRS. CRATCHIT.　You know it yourself, Robert, none better.

CRATCHIT (*pacifying her*).　My dear !

MRS. CRATCHIT (*relenting*).　Well, I'll drink his health for your sake, and the Day's.

CRATCHIT.　Good.

MRS. CRATCHIT.　But not for his. (*Sarcastically.*) A Merry Christmas and a Happy New Year ! He'll be happy and merry enough, I don't doubt.

CRATCHIT.　Never mind. (*He offers a toast.*) To Mr. Scrooge !

EVERYONE.　Mr. Scrooge !

(*They drink. There is a loud knock at the door.*)

MRS. CRATCHIT.　Why, who's that, I wonder ?

CRATCHIT (*putting his mug of punch on the mantelpiece*). Soon see. (*He crosses to the door and opens it.* SCROOGE *is standing on the threshold. But it is the old* SCROOGE, *menacing and disagreeable.*) Mr. Scrooge !

(*Everyone exclaims in consternation. Then they are silent.*)

TINY TIM (*suddenly*).　He's got two legs and he makes grunting noises.

MARTHA.　Ssh !

SCROOGE (*testy*).　Well, may I come in, or am I to be allowed to freeze on the doorstep ?

CRATCHIT (*stepping back hastily to admit him*).　Yes, of course, sir. I'm very sorry.

SCROOGE (*entering to* L.C.).　Hmm ! Sorry, he says.

(*There is an uneasy pause.*)

CRATCHIT (*moving to* L. *of* SCROOGE ; *lamely*). We were just—er—making merry, sir.

SCROOGE. So I see ! (*Fiercely.*) Now, look here, Cratchit !

MRS. CRATCHIT (*angrily*). It's not right . . .

MARTHA (*warning her*). Shh, Mama !

SCROOGE. I've just been looking through my account books, Cratchit.

CRATCHIT (*miserably*). Yes, sir. There's nothing wrong, I hope.

SCROOGE. Wrong ! There's something wrong all right. It won't do, Cratchit. It won't do. I'll not stand it any longer.

CRATCHIT. Is there a mistake, sir ?

SCROOGE. A grave one. I've just been looking at the amount of money I've been paying you each week. And it can't go on.

CRATCHIT (*terrified*). Can't go on, sir ?

SCROOGE. No. Therefore I have decided to—(*he makes a terrible pause*)—to raise your salary immediately.

CRATCHIT (*faintly*). Raise it ?

SCROOGE (*jovially*). Double it ! Starting today ! (*He seizes* CRATCHIT'S *hand and shakes it.*) A Merry Christmas, Bob, a merrier Christmas than I've given you for many a year.

CRATCHIT (*dreaming*). Thank you, sir.

SCROOGE. Now, I wonder if I might sit down for a moment, and we can discuss how I can best help you and your family.

CRATCHIT (*coming to life*). Yes, sir. Of course. Peter, a glass for Mr. Scrooge !

(PETER *pours a glass of punch for* MR. SCROOGE.)

Over there by the fire, sir. You'll take something to warm you ?

(SCROOGE *crosses below the table to the fireplace.*)

SCROOGE (*taking the glass of punch from* PETER). Thank you, thank you. (*He turns to* MRS. CRATCHIT.) Mrs. Cratchit, may I offer you and your children the best wishes of the Season ! (*He toasts them.*) To you all ! God Bless you !

MRS. CRATCHIT. You'll stay to dinner, Mr. Scrooge ? We're just about to have it.

SCROOGE (*sitting in the armchair*). Delighted. What a splendid fire ! We must have more like this at the office, Bob.

CRATCHIT. Yes. Mr. Scrooge, I'd like to thank you . . .

SCROOGE. No, no. I won't hear of it.

TINY TIM (*suddenly*). I want to get down.

MRS. CRATCHIT. In a minute.

TINY TIM (*loudly*). No. Now !

MARTHA (*rising to fetch his crutch from the sideboard*). Let him, Mama. (*She brings him the crutch.*)

(*She and* CRATCHIT *help* TINY TIM *to his feet. Slowly and in complete silence he crosses to* MR. SCROOGE *and stands looking at him.*)

TINY TIM (*after a pause ; casually*). I *like* you.

(SCROOGE *suddenly puts his arm round him and draws him close.*)

I'm Tiny Tim !

SCROOGE (*quietly*). I know. I know all about you.

(CRATCHIT *and* MRS. CRATCHIT *exchange glances.*)

TINY TIM. I know all about you, too. You've got two legs and you make grunt . . .

MRS. CRATCHIT (*hastily*). Now, Tiny Tim, you mustn't worry Mr. Scrooge.

SCROOGE. He's not. (*To* TINY TIM.) Here, sit on my knee. It's a bit boney, but never mind.

(*He helps* TINY TIM *on to his knees.*)

TINY TIM (*chatty*). It's Christmas today.

SCROOGE. Yes.

TINY TIM. They were singing carols this morning. Do you know any carols ?

SCROOGE. Well, I knew one once . . .

TINY TIM. Sing it now !

SCROOGE. What ! Me sing !

TINY TIM. Yes.

SCROOGE. Oh, I couldn't. I haven't sung since I was—well, I've forgotten, it was so long ago.

TINY TIM. Please sing a carol.

(*Everyone murmurs encouragement.*)

SCROOGE. All right ! I will !

(*General applause.*)

Mind you, it'll be a bit rusty at first. You'll have to help me.

(*They all encourage him.*)

All right, then. Here we go !

(SCROOGE *begins to sing " The First Noel" in a weak, uncertain voice.* TINY TIM *takes it up and all the* CRATCHITS *join in.* PETER *goes round with the jug and refills the glasses. As the carol reaches its climax, they lift their glasses and toast* SCROOGE, *with a burst of excited laughter and chatter. Suddenly* PETER *holds up his hand for silence.*)

PETER. Listen ! What's that ?

(*In the silence, the sound of " Come, all ye Faithful " is heard from outside the front door.*)

PETER. It's the waits !

(*There is great excitement and the* CRATCHITS *call to* PETER *to let them in. He crosses to the door down* L. *and admits the* WAITS, *who enter singing and fill the* L. *side of the stage. They include the* TWO PORTLY GENTLEMEN, *the* THREE BUSINESS GENTLEMEN *and* FRED, SCROOGE'S *nephew.*)

The CRATCHITS *and* SCROOGE *join in the carol. As it ends the* WAITS *raise their hats and the* CRATCHITS *and* SCROOGE *lift their mugs and glasses in a salute, as—*

the CURTAIN *falls.*

FURNITURE AND PROPERTY PLOT

PROLOGUE.

On Stage: Down R. Small wing armchair. *On it :* Cushion, copy of ' A Christmas Carol.'

Personal : BOY : wooden sword, paper hat.
FIRST GIRL : balloon, paper hat.
SECOND GIRL : paper hat.

ACT I

On Stage : On floor : Faded threadbare carpet.
Down R. Small mahogany chair.
Up R. : Faded blue curtains and pelmet to window.
Brass bell on bracket, with trick wire.
Up C. : Portrait of MARLEY.
Single mahogany chair.
Up L. : Large mahogany cupboard, containing six bags of coins, large cash box of loose coins, bottle of sherry and two glasses, pile of account books, ledgers.
On mantelpiece down L. : candle in candlestick, black marble clock, pewter mug with quill pens, pile of account books, loose papers.

In fireplace down L. : heavy iron dogs, fire-irons, practical electric fire, brass scuttle of coals, pewter mug with tapers.

R. of fireplace : wing armchair.

C. : flat-topped desk. *On it :* pen tray, quill pen, inkpot, ledgers, papers, candle in candlestick, open accounts book, small cash box, coins, tumbler.

L. of desk : mahogany chair.

R. of desk : mahogany chair.

Off stage down R. : account book (BOB CRATCHIT), stick and loose coins (FRED), papers (TWO PORTLY GENTLEMEN), long chain with ledgers, cash boxes and account books attached to it (MARLEY'S GHOST).

ACT II

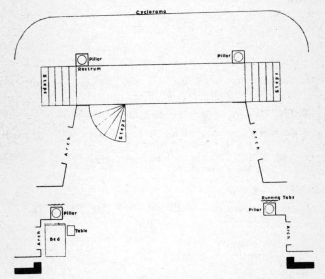

On Stage : Down R. : small bed, with a tall red canopy at up stage end. *On it :* pillows, sheets, blankets.
L. of bed : small table. *On it :* SCROOGE'S watch, extinguished candle in candlestick.

Personal : SPIRIT OF CHRISTMAS PAST : practical lamp on head, large candle extinguisher.

FIRST VISION.

> DANIEL : rough stick.
> FARMER and MRS. GREENROW : bunches of holly.
> SMALL BOY : tin trunk with E. SCROOGE painted on it.
> FEZZIWIG : watch and papers.

SECOND VISION (FEZZIWIG's house.)

On Stage :   up C. : decorated table. *On it :* punch bowl and ladle, glasses.
Up L. : small sofa.
Up R. : gilt chair, screen.

Personal :   FEZZIWIG : small jewel box containing brooch.

THIRD VISION.

Personal :   TINY TIM : crutch.
FIRST COCKNEY : bag of bottles.
SECOND COCKNEY : parcels.

FOURTH VISION.

On Stage :   L.C. : wing armchair, small table with bottle of sherry and two glasses.

FIFTH VISION. (The Churchyard.)

On Rostrum :   cemetery railings, large tombstone with SCROOGE illumination, small cross.

Personal :   BOB CRATCHIT : bunch of flowers.
MRS. CRATCHIT : bunch of flowers.

SIXTH VISION.

On Stage :   Down L. : small table with three chairs. *On it :* papers.

ACT III
SCENE 1

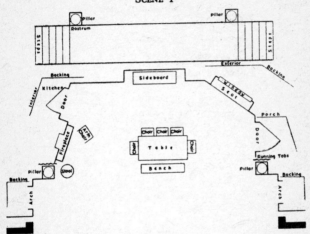

On Stage :   Lamp post.

Personal :   LAD : straw.
             SCROOGE : coins, cigars in pocket.
             TWO PORTLY GENTLEMEN : lists of contributors.
             FRED : cigars in case and matches.

SCENE 2

On Stage :   Up L. : window seat covered in chintz. *On it :*
             three cushions.
             Up C. : sideboard. *On it :* pewter mugs and plates,
             Toby jug, crockery, small Christmas tree, box
             of coloured bricks, eggcup, china mugs.
             Down R. on mantelpiece : china ornaments, three
             china mugs.
             In fireplace down R. : pile of logs, fire-irons, jug of
             punch.
             Below fireplace : small wooden stool.
             In front of hearth : rag rug.
             L. of hearth : Windsor armchair.
             C. : dining table laid with seven places, two mugs
             in centre and carving things at left.
             Above table : three Windsor chairs.

R. and L. of table : Windsor chairs.
Below table : wooden bench.

Personal :   MARTHA : cloak and bonnet.
TINY TIM : crutch.
BOB CRATCHIT : scarf.

Off R. :   Bread board and loaf (MRS. CRATCHIT)
Off L. :   Sheet music (WAITS).

EFFECTS

ACT I

Wind, clanking chains, tolling bell.

ACT II

Clock chime. (Four quarters and ONE). Clock chime. (Four quarters and TWELVE).

MUSIC

ACT I

" Good King Wenceslas."
" God rest you merry, Gentlemen."
Fortissimo passage of music for MARLEY's entance.

ACT II

" Sir Roger de Coverley."
" Hark, the Herald Angels Sing ! "
" Come all ye Faithful."

ACT III

"The First Noel " (sung on stage).
"Come all ye Faithful " (sung on stage).

LIGHTING PLOT

PROLOGUE :

Opening light : The CURTAIN rises in darkness.

Cue 1 :   *On* last phrase of " Good King Wenceslas," bring up general warm forestage lighting.

Cue 2 :   *On* " Come and sit round me," take out all lighting except the firelight spot on the armchair down R.

ACT I

Cue 3 :   *On* " . . . grasping, scraping, covetous old sinner," bring up a spotlight on SCROOGE at his desk.

Cue 4 :   *After* " . . . counting his money," take out firelight spot on armchair down R.

Cue 5 :   *On* exit of WOMAN and CHILDREN, bring up the general lighting in SCROOGE's office.

Cue 6 :   *When* SCROOGE lights the candles on his desk and on the mantelpiece, bring up candle spotlights.

Cue 7 :   *On* the entrance of the PORTLY GENTLEMEN, begin a slow fade-down of the general office lighting.

Cue 8 :   *When* SCROOGE puts out the candles, take out the candle spotlights.

Cue 9 :   *On* the entrance of MARLEY, switch on the green following spot.

Cue 10 :   *On* MARLEY's exit, take out the green following spot.

Cue 11 :   *When* SCROOGE re-lights the candles, bring up the candle spotlights.

ACT II

(NOTE : The Traverse Curtain is closed at the beginning of this Act. Sky-lighting for the first rostrum scene should be pre-set during the interval.)

Opening lighting : The CURTAIN rises in darkness.

Cue 1 :   *On* the last phrase of " While Shepherds Watched," bring up a spotlight on the bed down R.

Cue 2 :   *On* " the hour—and nothing else," set off flashbox in the footlights, and bring up a following pink spot for the SPIRIT OF CHRISTMAS PAST.

Cue 3 :   *On* " All right, I'm coming " (SCROOGE), take out the spotlight on the bed down R. (The Traverse Curtain opens.)

Cue 4 :   *As* SCROOGE sets his foot on the rostrum, bring up radiant sunset lighting on to and across the rostrum.

Cue 5 :   *On* " A little boy. His friends had forgotten him," bring up a spotlight on the SMALL BOY L.C.

Cue 6 :   *On* " It's too late now," take out the spotlight on the SMALL BOY L.C.

Cue 7 :   *On* "MR. FEZZIWIG's. I was apprenticed there," bring up a spotlight on MR. FEZZIWIG R.C.

Cue 8 :   *On* " Poor Dick ! Poor Dick ! ", fade out all cyclorama and rostrum lighting.

Cue 9 :   *As* MR. FEZZIWIG begins his mime sequence, bring up general lighting on main stage area.

Cue 10 :   *As* the Traverse Curtain closes behind MR. FEZZIWIG, bring up the forestage lighting.

(Pre-set lighting for next main scene behind the closed Traverse Curtain.)

Cue 11 :   *When* the Traverse Curtain opens, bring up bright general lighting for the Party Scene.

Cue 12 :   *At* the end of the dance, Black-Out.

Cue 13 :   *As soon as* the Traverse Curtain is closed, bring up spotlights down R. and C. of the forestage.

Cue 14 :   *As* SCROOGE enters with the SPIRIT OF CHRISTMAS PAST, switch on the pink following spot for the SPIRIT.

Cue 15 :   *On* " Haunt me no longer. Go ! Go ! ", as SCROOGE douses the SPIRIT's light, Black-Out.

Cue 16 :   *As soon as* the SPIRIT OF CHRISTMAS PAST is off, bring up spotlights down R. and C. of the forestage.

Cue 17 :   *During* the first section of " Hark, the Herald Angels Sing," slowly increase the level of the forestage lighting to a bright morning light.

Cue 18 :   *During* the middle section of the carol, slowly increase the forestage lighting to full.

Cue 19 :   *During* the closing part of the carol, slowly reduce the general lighting to Cue 16 level.

Cue 20 :   *At* the entry of the SPIRIT OF CHRISTMAS PRESENT, switch on a following red spot.

Cue 21 :   *On* " Come then !", as the Traverse Curtain opens, take out the forestage lighting and bring up the sky lighting on the main stage.

Cue 22 :   *As* the FIRST COCKNEY enters on the rostrum, bring up bright sunshine across the rostrum.

Cue 23 :   *On* " None can help you but yourself," bring up a spotlight on the armchair L.C. and a fire-flood through the arch L.C.

Cue 24 :   *On* " and a Happy New Year to the old gentleman, wherever he is," take out the spotlight and fire-flood L.C.

Cue 25 :   *On* " Can't I stay and hear a bit more ? ", fade out all lights except the red following spot.

Cue 26 :   *On* " Remember the ignorant, remember the sick . . .", slowly fade the red following spot to out.

Cue 27 :   *When* the SPIRIT OF CHRISTMAS PRESENT is off stage, bring up a spotlight on the bed down R.

Cue 28 :   *When* the SPIRIT OF CHRISTMAS YET TO COME enters, switch on a white following spot.

Cue 29 :   *On* " Then lead and I will follow," fade out the spotlight on the bed down R., and bring in cyclorama lighting.

Cue 30 :   *On* " And He took a child and set him in the midst of them," bring up spotlights across the rostrum.

Cue 31 :   *On* " Only your heart can tell you," bring up a spotlight on the forestage down L.

Cue 32 :   *On* " After all, he is dead ! ", take out the spotlight on the forestage down L.

Cue 33 :   *As* SCROOGE approaches the gravestone, switch on the tombstone effect.

Cue 34 :   *On* " No, no, no ! ", as the SPIRIT OF CHRISTMAS YET TO COME goes off, switch off the white following spot.

Cue 35 :   *During* the carol " Come all ye Faithful," increase the rostrum and cyclorama lighting to full, and slowly fade out the tombstone effect.

ACT III

SCENE 1

Opening light : A cold, bright, frosty morning.

Cue 1 :   Black-Out.

SCENE 2

Standing Lighting : Bright, warm interior lighting.

SUGGESTED DOUBLING OF PARTS IN THE PLAY

1. A Woman. Agnes. Martha Cratchit.
2. Boy. Scrooge as a boy. Tiny Tim.
3. 1st girl. Spirit of Christmas Past. Belinda.
4. 2nd girl. Emma Fezziwig. Sarah.
5. Ebeneezer Scrooge.
6. Bob Cratchit.
7. 1st Portly Gentleman. Mr. Fezziwig.
8. 2nd Portly Gentleman. Daniel. 1st Cockney.
9. Fred. Spirit of Christmas to Come.
10. Ghost of Marley. Marley as young man. 1st Business Man.
11. Farmer Greenrow. Adolphus.
12. Mrs. Greenrow. Mrs. Cratchit.
13. Dick Wilkins. Peter Cratchit.
14. Mrs. Fezziwig.
15. Dora.
16. Augusta.
17. Spirit of Christmas Present. 3rd Business Man.
18. 2nd Cockney. 2nd Business Man.
19. Lad.
20. Fanny Fezziwig.

MADE AND PRINTED IN GREAT BRITAIN BY
BUTLER & TANNER LTD, FROME AND LONDON

MADE IN ENGLAND